TRUMPETS
TO THE WEST

TRUMPETS TO THE WEST

WILL COOK

THORNDIKE
CHIVERS

This Large Print edition is published by Thorndike Press®, Waterville, Maine USA and by BBC Audiobooks, Ltd, Bath, England.

Published in 2004 in the U.S. by arrangement with Golden West Literary Agency.

Published in 2004 in the U.K. by arrangement with Golden West Literary Agency.

U.S. Hardcover 0-7862-6709-7 (Western)
U.K. Hardcover 1-4056-3044-2 (Chivers Large Print)
U.K. Softcover 1-4056-3045-0 (Camden Large Print)

The text of this Large Print edition is unabridged.
Other aspects of the book may vary from the original edition.

Set in 16 pt. Plantin by Ramona Watson.

Printed in the United States on permanent paper.

British Library Cataloguing-in-Publication Data available

Library of Congress Cataloging-in-Publication Data

Cook, Will.
    Trumpets to the west : a novel of the U.S. Cavalry in action / Will Cook.
        p. cm.
        ISBN 0-7862-6709-7 (lg. print : hc : alk. paper)
        1. Telegraph lines — Design and construction — Fiction.
2. United States. Army. Cavalry — Fiction.   3. Sabotage —
Fiction.   4. Soldiers — Fiction.   5. Large type books.
    I. Title.
PS3553.O5547T78 2004
    813′.54—dc22   2004049831

TRUMPETS
TO THE WEST

CHAPTER 1

All that day and into the night a slashing rain stippled the swart waters of the Hudson River, scuffed the surface of the drill field until it was a morass of mud, and tore in tormented fury around Central Barracks, driving all but the most hearty indoors. West Point, after tattoo, is quiet on any night, but now few stirred. In the commanding officer's quarters a light burned, flashing a feeble beacon through the rain-smeared window. At the corner of Jefferson Road and Thayer, two cadets plowed through the storm toward their barracks. Near the library a shower of lamplight layered the wet lawn and rain rattled at the windows as a handful of cadets boned for the never-ceasing examinations. The library served as a sanctuary after tattoo, for a cadet was not permitted to absent himself from the barracks except for study. There were no guards. Under the severe honor system, cadets reported themselves for the slightest infraction of rules.

The main door of the library opened, allowing a boxed shaft of light to blare forth, then closed, leaving the high columned porch in shocking darkness. Cadet Captain Quincy St. Clair lingered a moment, pondering his next move.

The commandant had stopped him earlier in the day with an odd message: "Cadet, will you accept an unusual order? Good. Report to my quarters tonight after tattoo. Don't get caught."

Don't get caught. . . .

He wondered how he was going to manage this.

Clutching his long cape close about him, St. Clair stepped from the porch into the driving rain. Behind the library, the gray sandstone chapel rose in quiet strength against the beating weather. St. Clair took sanctuary against the ivy-covered wall, shrinking back in an alcove where the wind was less piercing. For two miserable minutes he hesitated, going over a course of action in his mind. He decided that boldness should carry him through, for if he were challenged he could offer most any excuse and have it accepted.

Abandoning the dark shelter of the chapel, St. Clair scurried across the sodden lawn, turned right on Thayer Road and walked rapidly north until he came to Jefferson. Then he crossed the graveled drive to hug the haven of trees bordering the south and west edges of the Plain. The wind was not so harsh here and he hurried, both from a desire not to be seen and the urge to leave this vile weather. His clothes were completely wet by the time he passed Central Barracks and made the bend to the northwest toward the commandant's house. He walked with his head at a list to battle the wind-whipped rain. The hedge masked his movement, but he paused twice, searching the dark road behind to see if he were being followed. Directly across from the commandant's house St. Clair paused again, then dashed across the street, made a circular sweep around the house and emerged on an obscure garden path that led to the rear door. To the east and on his left now the Hudson River boiled on, tormented by the downpour.

St. Clair raised his knuckles and rapped on the door.

He was admitted almost immediately. The kitchen was dark. Across the room a door opened into a hall, and lamplight glowed on the waxed floor from yet another room. He had heard the murmur of men's voices when he stepped inside, but then came a sudden hush.

The colored servant said, "This way,

suh," and preceded him into the commandant's drawing room. He saw two men beside the commandant. They looked at Cadet Captain St. Clair and continued to gnaw on their cigars.

Major Delafield, the commandant, rose and St. Clair came to a stiff position of attention. St. Clair was the precise six feet that the Academy liked. His face was long and slightly pointed from the sharp cheekbones down — a scholar's face — but in the pale gray of his eyes there lurked the hint of a fighter. The uniform cast St. Clair in prim identity with the other four hundred and eighty-one men at the Academy. He wore the crossed, pipe-clayed belts of the cadet, three rows of brass buttons down his tunic, and the high leather hat with the plume. Boots, white gloves, and the full length weather cape dripping water on the commandant's rug, added to his soldierly bearing.

Major Delafield said, "When I was last in New York, your father asked me to convey his respects to you."

"Thank you, sir," St. Clair said from the cadet position of attention, which does not permit the slightest movement.

The colored servant lingered at the door and Major Delafield said, "Prepare a toddy

10

for Mr. St. Clair, then leave us, Mose."

"Yassah," Mose said, and shuffled toward the kitchen.

The two men with Major Delafield measured Cadet St. Clair with their eyes. Major Delafield settled himself in a soft chair and crossed his legs. His heavy brows threw shadows around his eyes. His mustache drooped on each side of his mouth and his side whiskers were gray balls of cotton. Mose returned with the hot drink and Delafield said, "At ease, Mister. You can't drink at attention."

St. Clair moved his left foot precisely ten inches to the rear of his right and took the drink. His eyes were watering slightly when he handed back the empty mug to Mose and a core of flame had settled in his stomach.

"Take Mr. St. Clair's cape, Mose, then close the study door."

"Yassuh," Mose said, and went out.

"Have you ever seen these gentlemen before?" Major Delafield asked. His dark, piercing eyes skewered St. Clair and held him like a bug on the end of a pin.

"No, sir. I have never seen them before, sir."

Delafield leaned back and placed his fist in his palm. "Perhaps you find it strange

11

that you should be summoned here in this manner."

"Indeed I do, sir. Most strange."

"Mister, I want to ask you a few questions. I'll require quick answers on decisions of the utmost importance. There's no time for dilly-dallying. The honest answer is the one I want. Do you understand?"

"Yes, sir."

"This is Mr. Wade Garland," Delafield said, indicating the big man in an expensive coat. Garland's face was square, made more so by his beard trimmed straight across just above the collar. His eyebrows were dark thickets over his eyes. He merely nodded and continued to puff his cigar. "— And Mr. Alex Howison," Major Delafield concluded.

Howison was not big; neither was he impressive. He had an unruly mane of taffy-colored hair and although he wore a fine suit, it appeared wrinkled and ill-fitting on his spare frame.

"These gentlemen may ask you questions at random," Delafield said.

"How old are you?" Garland asked. His voice was soft but St. Clair felt power behind it, power and the authority developed through years of command.

"Twenty-two, sir."

"Is Humphrey A. St. Clair your father?"

"Yes."

"Don't I know him?" Howison asked Garland. He spoke around his cigar and his voice had a slight lisp because of this.

"He's a New York banker," Garland said. "You met him once at the Stuyvesant Club."

"Yaaah," Howison said and removed his cigar. He looked directly at Cadet St. Clair. "The man struck me as being a swindler," he said.

The color drained from Quincy St. Clair's face and for a moment he held his breath. He threw his balance forward to take a step toward Howison. Major Delafield snapped, "TENSH-HUT!"

St. Clair's heels clicked. Once again he was a statue.

"If you have an answer," Major Delafield said sternly, "be so kind as to deliver it from the position of attention."

St. Clair said, "Sir, since this gentleman has chosen a most inopportune time to insult me, I am compelled to await one more fitting in which to rectify Mr. Howison's error." He moved his eyes then and locked them with Alex Howison's. "I shall await your seconds, sir. The choice of weapons is yours."

Alex Howison glanced at Wade Garland and smiled. "Nervy, isn't he?" He looked at St. Clair again. "You'll have to forgive me. Your father is one of my closest friends. I apologize."

"I — I don't understand," St. Clair said.

"Have you ever hated a man?" Garland asked.

"Yes, sir."

"You dislike Cadet Major Niles Upton," Delafield said. "At ease, Mister. Three times you've settled differences behind the rifle butts. Why do you dislike Upton?"

"He's too ostentatious, sir."

"Ostentatious?" Howison said. "Explain that." He leaned forward in his chair, his forefinger curled around the cigar in his mouth.

"He has a very good opinion of himself, sir. I've always believed that this attitude will prove harmful after he receives his commission."

"I understand," Garland said. "Are you in love, Mr. St. Clair?"

"I think so, sir. I'm engaged."

"You think so?" Major Delafield said. "Don't you know, Mister?"

"I'm afraid I'm rather inclined to treat romance lightly, sir," St. Clair said seriously. "When I was seventeen I fell in and

14

out of love every month."

"But you say you're engaged," Delafield pointed out. "That's a serious step for a young man so uncertain."

"An engagement isn't irrevocable, sir, and with my future destination still undetermined, I'm sure the young lady in question holds the same view."

"I see," Delafield said, and stroked his mustache. "I hadn't considered it in quite that light. Mister St. Clair, are you interested in politics?"

"Yes, sir. I am."

"Do you think there will be a war between the North and the South?" Garland asked.

Quincy St. Clair paused. "Shall I be completely honest, sir?"

"What other kind of honesty is there?" Garland asked.

"I believe there will be a war unless Washington politics change, and I hold small hope for that."

"How do you feel about the slavery issue?" Howison wanted to know.

"I fail to see it as the main issue," St. Clair said. "If there is armed conflict, it will be because of the high prices the South is obliged to pay for the sake of protecting Northern industry. The South will probably start the war, but I think the North, unfortunately, will be responsible for it."

"I see your father hasn't neglected your education in basic economics," Howison said with a smile.

"I've heard enough, Major," Garland said. "He'll do."

Major Delafield placed his hands together and said, "Mister St. Clair, would you be greatly shocked if I asked you to desert the United States Military Academy when your graduation is only a week away?"

"I — yes! Why would I do a thing like that, sir?"

"To serve your country in a greater capacity than you could ever serve her as a lieutenant of cavalry."

"Then I would, sir," St. Clair said.

"Would you become a deserter, forsaking family, fiancee — all this for the love of duty?" Delafield was driving this home with hammer blows.

Cadet St. Clair bit his lip and looked from one man to the other. They were watching him gravely, expectantly. He wondered if they understood what they were asking of him. His father would go to his study to open Major Delafield's carefully worded message — his father always retired to the oak-paneled study to review unpleasantness, whether it was a decline in the market or the reprimanding of his slightly wayward son — and his father's face would be rigid with control, the lips stern, the eyes carefully veiled against the possibility of his thoughts bleeding through.

This would be no different, St. Clair thought, from the other times he had been disciplined, except that he would not be present to receive his father's wrath or the stunned grief of his mother. No different from the time he had used the alderman's brake to take the neighbor girl riding in the park, or his withdrawal from that up-state military prep school — a withdrawal that preceded his dismissal by an hour.

His father had been very displeased then while his mother had cried and wrung her hands, certain that her only son was headed for disgrace.

The vision of willful, lovely Glorianna flitted before him. His father would have disapproved of her anyway; long ago he had made up his mind to that. The elder St. Clair had indicated many times that when the time was ripe for marriage he would personally select the proper girl from the social register. . . .

Finally St. Clair said, "If I must, sir."

"There is no must about this, Mister," Delafield said. "It's strictly volunteer. But I must have your solemn word now, before I can tell you more."

"May I ask why I was selected, sir?"

"Won't hurt to tell him," Garland said softly, and kindled a fresh cigar.

Delafield nodded. "St. Clair, you stand at the top of your class, academically, but as a disciplinarian I can vouch for the fact that you're hot-headed, stubborn, willful, and within a hair's breadth of having sufficient demerits to expel you. Every man in your family has served as an officer in the military service, and all with distinction. Personally, I believe you came here because of tradition rather than personal choice, but I believe you've grown fond of the service. You are the man for this job."

"May I ask —"

"You may not," Delafield said. "No more will be said until I have your sworn word that you're prepared to follow out my orders to the letter."

Cadet Captain Quincy St. Clair considered this for a full minute while Garland and Howison waited with mounting impatience. "I consent," he said at last. "I

18

give you my word as a future officer and a gentleman, providing I have a future."

Delafield was visibly relieved. He left his chair to pace back and forth across the room. Finally he paused before a large wall map. "Mr. Garland and Mr. Howison are the engineers for the newly formed Western Union Telegraph Company. Their job is to push a line of communication through to the west coast. The Union must have California and Oregon. Politicians are at work now trying to get a statehood for Nevada Territory. Nevada silver and gold is badly needed.

"But this isn't our immediate problem, Mister. Our problem is the split loyalty within the service. We have officers — yes, field grade officers — who are in sympathy with the Southern cause. The army is supposed to guard the telegraph workers while they string their wires, but so far we have not yet completed the surveying. There have been betrayals, labor shortages, equipment sabotage, Indian troubles — and this has to be stopped or we'll never get a line through."

"I don't understand my part, sir," St. Clair said.

Delafield smiled. "We have a damn small army, St. Clair, and when I say 'army' I'm

19

speaking of the officer corps." He paused to let this sink in. "Let me put it to you this way, mister — I need a spy. I can't use an enlisted man simply because he lacks the training and wouldn't think in the manner of command function. I'm afraid my only choice must be an officer." He spread his hands. "But what officer? As I said, the corps is small and they all know each other, even the newest graduates of the Academy. So you can see how my decision came around to you. A West Point man about to graduate, an officer in every sense, but having the perfect cover of not being an officer on the register. No one will know you, mister. At least not in the capacity I would most fear, as an officer."

"Major Delafield is being polite," Howison said. "What he means is, you'll be considered a deserter and no other officer will care about you. It may be that you'll have a rough time getting on with the enlisted men also."

For a moment Cadet St. Clair looked like a man who was sorry he had made a promise. "What will I have to do, sir?"

Delafield smiled and pulled the bell cord to summon his servant. Mose came in and Delafield said, "Do as I instructed you earlier. Do it now."

"Yes, suh!" He hurried out and a moment later the front door slammed.

From his desk drawer, Major Delafield took a Navy Colt pistol, a small wallet, and a folded issue raincape. "Remove your uniform at your barracks," he said. "Here's ninety dollars and a pistol and see that you lose neither of them. I've sent Mose to find Cadet Major Upton. You'll leave here in exactly seven minutes." He glanced at his turnip watch. "Nearly eleven. Carry this raincoat, or wear it. It's a badge that will be recognized while you're traveling west. When you leave here, walk boldly down the walk. You'll run into Upton. You'll be out of bounds and in trouble. He'll put you on report." Delafield smiled. "Being on report will be no new experience for you, Mister.

"Then go to your barracks and change into civilian clothes. Leave the post immediately. You'll have to get out without being seen by the sentry. A mile down the road there'll be a barn with a horse in it, just waiting for you to steal. In Cornwall, you'll find that a stage leaves at four o'clock in the morning. That'll give you time to catch the train at Newburgh. Go straight through to Jefferson Barracks and enlist."

21

"Will my father know the truth about this?" St. Clair asked. "My fiancee, Glorianna Holland?"

"No," Delafield said flatly. "To the world you'll be a deserter. But there'll be a few who'll know the truth. When you get on the train, you'll eventually be joined by a Sergeant Delaney. Make no move to question him until he speaks of the pistol or raincoat." Delafield glanced at his watch again. "Better get going, Mister." He offered his hand. "Good luck and be careful. This is more than a game."

"Yes, sir," St. Clair said. He shook hands with Wade Garland and Alex Howison.

"We'll see you on the frontier," Garland said. "You'll be contacted and instructed farther down the line. Remember that part about being careful, St. Clair. We've lost two excellent officers already. You're out there alone and you're our last hope."

"I'll do my best, gentlemen," St. Clair said. He followed Major Delafield down the hall to the door. The lamps had been turned down and when St. Clair stepped out onto the porch, darkness was a cloak that enveloped him quickly. The door shut and he was committed to a course that had no certain ending.

Moving along the darkened path, Quincy

St. Clair thought of Glorianna Holland's reaction when she received the news, and the knowledge that she probably would condemn him was a weight on his spirit. She loved him; he felt sure of that. But would love be enough to overbalance the uncertainty of youth?

How could he expect her to understand? A person needed some shred of truth to cling to, but Major Delafield would conceal all but the most damning evidence. To the world at large he would be fleeing because he had been caught in the infraction that would bring his total to dismissal. He was cleanly cut off, now, and he felt a sharp regret.

The wind rocked St. Clair. The rain wove a new chill around him. But he did not have long to worry. A shadow loomed ahead on the path and a man shouted, "Halt! Identify yourself!"

Crouching, St. Clair waited until Cadet Major Upton was no more than ten feet from him, then hurled himself in a driving plunge, ramming Upton solidly in the chest with his shoulder. For a grim moment they embraced and grappled, their boots sucking at the mud along the path. Quincy St. Clair took a blow to the head that knocked his hat to the ground and fell back a step, his feet losing purchase in the rain-slick lawn. He made a weak counter charge and Niles Upton smashed him in the chest with a stiffened arm.

"Stand and be recognized!" Upton shouted and St. Clair ceased struggling. Upton's hand went inside his cape and came out with a match. In the sudden blob of brightness before the wind whipped it out, Upton's face was deeply shadowed, but gloating. "You're at attention!" he said. "Explain your presence here and this attack upon a classman!"

"I decline to explain, sir — respectfully."

"Very well," Upton said. He was a year older than St. Clair. He had blond hair, worn long, and his eyes were dark with anger. "Out of bounds! Out of uniform! Mose said he saw a man lurking near the Parade. Return to your barracks and report yourself in the morning, Mister."

Head down, St. Clair wheeled and disappeared into the rainy night.

What was it he had to do now? Oh, yes. Change his clothes and get past the north gate without getting caught.

That shouldn't be difficult on a night like this. The cadet guard would be snug inside the sentry box.

Niles would report to the old man immediately, make a big stink — which was what the commandant wanted.

The major's shrewdness impressed St. Clair. Without leaving his warm study, Delafield would know that Stage One had been passed as soon as Cadet Upton made his report.

St. Clair hurried on to carry off Stage Two: His escape from the Academy. Without being told, he knew that if he bobbled this, Delafield would dismiss him from the Academy in truth, without honor. He had no alternative but to carry on.

CHAPTER 2

Cadet Major Niles Upton had always found time and reason for self congratulation. On this occasion he began by reminding himself of his fine-honed wits, disregarding the possibility that luck could have brought about this night's work.

Ambition was Upton's strongest motivation. For three years now he had tried to best St. Clair and rise to honor position in the class, but somehow St. Clair always managed to keep that pace between them that made Niles Upton number two. A man graduated at the head of his class was slated for great things. Men of rank scanned the grades carefully and the high student was almost in a position to accept bids. Choosing his arm or service, even his unit and kind of duty. He had the close attention of his superiors, and usually gained the first promotion.

Niles Upton desired all these things.

But the classroom was not the only place where St. Clair excelled. Cadet Upton reminded himself that Glorianna Holland had been solely his girl until Quincy St. Clair smiled her way. Stung by the insult of their ensuing engagement, he had set about undermining the alliance for his own satisfaction.

Fickle Glorianna had found it expedient to keep Cadet Upton as a clandestine lover.

Mose, had he arrived some five minutes later, would have missed Cadet Upton, who had a pressing engagement elsewhere. But Mose had not missed him and the night became uncommonly lucky. *Perhaps,* he thought, *I should report to Major Delafield. No. It can wait until morning.*

Cadet Upton beat a cautious path toward the Old Fort, taking care to keep well hidden, although there was little chance that anyone would be about on a night so foul. No one, that is, except Glorianna Holland. She would be drawn by the adventure of their secret tryst.

She was beautiful and ambitious, but really not his type at all. Her father was a nobody, a merchant in Highland Falls. But her company was stimulating and ego-satisfying and Upton enjoyed the feeling that he was stealing from Quincy St. Clair.

When he first met Glorianna, Upton had judged her to be timid. Away from prying

27

eyes, however, he had found her anything but shy.

Once inside the gate of the abandoned fort, Upton skirted to the side to evade the insistent rain. He moved more slowly to conceal his eagerness.

Women always attached such significance to these small things.

He found her a moment later, standing in a sheltered doorway, and drew her possessively into his arms. She gave him a lingering kiss. Then, feeling his withheld excitement, she drew back to look at him.

"St. Clair is in real trouble now," he said with some satisfaction.

Her reaction was guarded. "What kind?"

She doesn't seem too concerned, he thought. "I caught him out-of-bounds tonight on the commandant's grounds. This demerit is enough to dismiss him, you know." He smiled to himself. "Naturally, I'll report him. It's my duty."

Misinterpreting her silence, he kissed her again. She returned his ardor with abandon. Then she pushed against him until he released her.

"Where will they send you after graduation?" Her voice was mildly calculating.

"I don't know," he said, and thought, *Away from you, that's for sure. I'll have my revenge on both of you now.* "This little caper puts me at the head of the class. I think I'd like the Cavalry. A smart man can make a name for himself out West these days."

"I've heard that the frontier is very dangerous," Glorianna said skeptically. "Is it safe for an officer's wife?"

Officer's wife! Upton stiffened. *Good God, she thinks I'm going to marry her!* "We'd best discuss that after I'm commissioned," he said coolly. "Who knows? I may draw Washington."

"I'd like that," Glorianna said softly, and rewarded him with another kiss.

"I must be getting back," Upton declared.

She put her arms around his neck again. "Come to the house for dinner next week before you graduate. I shouldn't like it if you neglected me, Niles."

"That's silly talk," he said, with a pang of misgiving.

On returning to the post, Upton went first to St. Clair's barracks to have a talk with him. He entered, made his way carefully down the dark aisle, and stopped abruptly. St. Clair's bed was empty. The man's uniform was in a heap on the floor and the wall locker door stood open.

St. Clair had *deserted!*

Cadet Major Upton didn't know whether to be pleased or worried. His consternation gave way to the thought that some men seek punishment for their misdeeds. As a child he had often told on himself when his conscience was heavy, seeking the purifying sting of the razor strap. He recalled vividly the clean feeling that would flood him when he had done his penance in this fashion.

Upton returned to his own barracks and crawled into bed, pulling the heavy blankets snug around his neck. He listened to the storm blast the building, still splattering rain against the windows. Outside a man was running, a man afraid to face his own just punishment. The knowledge that St. Clair had proved himself to be morally weak pleased Upton, yet with the man gone, Glorianna Holland presented something of a problem. This would necessitate a change in his plans about her.

He would have to think of something.

Major Delafield consulted his watch at five minute intervals and his boots made a hushed scrape across the carpet. Howison and Garland exchanged glances, then Howison said, "Major, it's been over an hour and a half. Do you think something has gone wrong?"

"I don't know, gentlemen," Delafield admitted, and rang for Mose.

When the servant came into the room, Delafield asked, "Are you sure you contacted Mr. Upton?"

"Yassuh, I sho' did, suh. Mistah Upton he in his barrack' all dressed. I tole him what you tole me to tell him and he hurry out in de rain, suh."

"That's all, Mose. Go to bed now."

"Yassuh," Mose said and left.

Delafield stroked his mustache. "I can't understand why Upton didn't report to me." He gave a short laugh. "Gentlemen, my hands are tied. I dare not approach him; he must come to me. I was relying on his report as a check that St. Clair made the contact. Without this breach of regulations, he would have no apparent reason for leaving the Academy."

Garland rotated his cigar between his lips. "St. Clair would have come back if anything had gone wrong. He could be clear of the reservation right now."

"We'll have to assume that," Delafield said, "at least until we know otherwise."

Ex-Cadet Quincy St. Clair found the horse, made his stage connection and got

31

on the train at the commencement of another weeping day. Throughout the gray daylight he slept, bypassing the panorama of rain-soaked Pennsylvania and most of Ohio's rolling land. In Indiana he woke late at night when the train stopped, got off for a meal, and barely made it back in time before the train puffed out of the station.

Quincy St. Clair was beginning to look the part of a fugitive. He showed a quarter-inch beard and soot had grimed him, making dark lines in the folds of his skin. In the washroom he stripped to the waist, washed as well as he could, and returned to his seat.

A soldier and a young girl had settled themselves in the seat across from his. As he walked down the aisle he looked them over carefully. The man was a sergeant major, and from the hashmarks, had spent a lifetime in the service. In cavalry blues, the man wore a grizzled dignity. Heavy-boned, his face was blunt and Irish. His eyebrows were jet black although the hair at his temples was gray. He wore the popular sweeping mustaches, the hairs of which remained disciplined without wax.

The girl he judged to be the sergeant's daughter, for in feature and coloring he read a similarity. Her hair and eyes were dark, her mouth firm, and Quincy St. Clair was just fickle enough to regret being asleep when she had boarded the train.

When he reached his seat he paused, for another man was now sitting there, a large man in a buffalo coat. St. Clair had carefully laid his raincape on the seat to indicate previous ownership. Now it lay on the floor, flung there when the man cleared a place for himself.

Coming up past the sergeant's daughter, St. Clair said, "Excuse me, please," and tapped the man on the arm. "Pardon me, friend, but that's my seat you've taken."

"Is it now?" Buffalo Coat smiled around his cigar. He raised a pair of mild blue eyes to St. Clair, then dropped them to the raincape. "That yours too?"

"Yes," St. Clair told him evenly. "Now, if you don't mind —"

The train navigated a curve, gaining speed. St. Clair braced himself against the sway, his long legs spread. Buffalo Coat took the cigar from his mouth, and his smile broadened. "But I do mind. You'd best run along, lad, and hunt yourself another." The man wore an old pair of cavalry pants tucked into high boots. His eyes wrinkled with amusement as he watched St. Clair.

"I happen to like this one," St. Clair said, and bent, picking up his raincape. The oilskin garment was stiff now, and he shook it out patiently, refolding it tightly until it was six inches wide and three feet long. "I won't ask you to move again," he said softly.

"Now then, I'll be bettin' you won't either," Buffalo Coat said, his Irish brogue thick. "You're lookin' at the best man in County Kerry. Now move along with ye."

"My mother's from County Cork," St. Clair said and whipped the slicker across the man's face, leaving a bloody track where the cold-stiffened edge had cut in.

With an oath, Buffalo Coat exploded from the seat, and in his haste he cracked his head on the baggage rack. Without hesitation, St. Clair hit him, a driving blow that left the man's lips bruised and bleeding. The man went back against the coach wall and stayed there, wiping a hand across his lips. "Faith now," he said, " 'tis like the fair at Killarney when I was a lad."

The conductor hurried down the aisle and the other passengers turned in their seats to watch. The sergeant put out his hand when the conductor came up and said, "Easy now, Captain. It's between these two gentlemen and it wouldn't do to interfere."

Taking the easy way out, the conductor stepped back and Buffalo Coat came away from the coach wall, boring into St. Clair. Retreating slightly, St. Clair blocked a driving punch while the man's other hand pawed at him, ripping open his coat. Hitting him again, St. Clair swayed with the rock of the coach and felt a blow sting his cheek. Sensing an easy victory, the man rushed St. Clair, but St. Clair raised an elbow and let him run into it with his mouth. If he had rammed the blunt end of a four by four the effect could not have been more stunning, for St. Clair was no lightweight and four years in the Academy riding ring had reduced him to solid muscle.

St. Clair pelted the man on the eye, then laced a quick punch into his stomach. When the man gasped and bent over, St. Clair grabbed him by his hide collar and threw him headlong down the aisle.

Flinging the man's plunder after him, St. Clair said, "Make this easy on yourself now and find another seat."

Buffalo Coat sat up and wiped at the blood running from his nose. "Ah now," he said, "are you sure you're not from County Kerry yourself?"

St. Clair grinned and touched his bruised cheek, then sat down across from the sergeant and his daughter. The sergeant studied St. Clair for a moment, then said, "You play a rough game of knuckles, friend."

"So does he." St. Clair nodded toward Buffalo Coat, who was now sitting at the far end of the coach. The sergeant swung his eyes to the raincape, now laid out on the seat.

"What's the pistol for?" the girl asked and St. Clair stared at her. The softness of her voice reminded him of the chapel bells on a summer evening — tones so clear and low, yet seemingly able to carry across vast distances.

A glance down showed the butt of the Navy Colt jutting past his coat. He covered it and said, "A going-away present from my mother."

"You must have left in a hurry?" the girl said. "No luggage."

"Peg!" Her father spoke sharply.

"I know." She smiled. "Keep my nose out of other people's business. I'm sorry," she said to St. Clair, "but women are supposed to be notoriously nosy, aren't they?"

"No comment," St. Clair said, and was warmed by her smile.

The sergeant picked up St. Clair's raincape and turned it over in his hands. Then he leaned forward in the seat and said, "I'd be knowin' that pistol you're carryin'. Major Delafield owned a pistol like that. I think you'll find his name and date of presentation on the backstrap: Major H. C. Delafield, June 16, 1857."

St. Clair was amazed at the smoothness with which the contact had been made. The sergeant glanced at his daughter, then back to St. Clair. "You can speak in front of her."

"I'm Quincy St. Clair, if the name means anything to you."

"Sergeant Major Delaney. This is my daughter, Peg, Lieutenant, but for the sake of the ears that might be listenin', we'll call you Quincy — with your permission."

"I'm new at this," St. Clair said. "I'm not even sure I rate such a title, Sergeant."

"You've been commissioned," Delaney said. "A few at the top know it, but that's all." He paused to fill his pipe and light it. "I'm to stay with you. You'll enlist at Jefferson Barracks."

"Enlist? Do I have to do that?"

"There's no other way," Delaney said. He glanced at his daughter. "Why don't you go to sleep, lass, and let us talk?"

"Listening's more fun," she said, but she slumped in the seat.

Delaney sighed. "Quincy, the word's going to get out, purposely, that you deserted rather than face your punishment. That's all part of the plan to make everyone think you're disgraced. A few, like myself, will know better, but you'll enlist and no one will give a damn what you do after that as long as you soldier. You'll be in my outfit and the commanding officer will know the whole story. He'll see that you're placed where you'll do the most good."

"Cavalry?"

Delaney nodded. "I'm Cavalry. The trouble's in Kansas and beyond. Western Union has to string wire across the continent, but they'll never do it with all the trouble they've been havin'. The Eighth Colorado is stationed at Fort Scott, but they're goin' on to Ellsworth and the Smoky Hill country. There's been trouble with the Ogallala Sioux. Our main job is to keep the hostiles in check while the wire goes through. They've got to complete the job by fifty-nine and they have a long way to go."

"What am I supposed to do?" St. Clair asked.

"The Army's full of Southern sympathizers. They cause trouble. It's your job to watch out for these men, then point them out so they can be taken care of." He paused to puff on his pipe. "This is a dangerous mission, no mistake. Two good officers have been killed, just listenin'."

"I'm going to try to stay alive," St. Clair said. He grinned. "I'm too young to die."

Peg Delaney watched St. Clair with more frankness than was common in a girl. He decided that he liked it. At first she had seemed unusually pretty, but upon closer inspection he altered his opinion. Her nose was too delicate for beauty, and her lips too long to balance a face that tapered to a pert chin. Her dress did not completely conceal a body that was boyishly slim, with small breasts pouting her bodice. Her hips were slender, her waist so small he could have spanned it with his hands. Yet he sensed a fine-honed strength in her.

She wasn't at all like Glorianna Holland . . . *Glorianna!* He hadn't thought of her for many hours and the shock of it made him feel like a traitor.

"You look like a man who's just swallowed his tobacco," Peg said.

The remark caught Quincy completely off balance.

"I was thinking about a girl in Highland

Falls," he said too quickly. "Wondering how she's taking the news of my — ah, desertion."

"She either believes in you and is calling everyone a liar or she's coasting along with public opinion. In the latter case, you'll have to find yourself another, won't you?"

"That's enough!" Delaney snapped irritably. "How many times do I have to tell you to keep your sharp tongue off people?"

"I'll never learn," she said. She appeared contrite, but St. Clair knew that she wasn't.

"She's been listenin' to me talk to the troop," Delaney said. "An Army post is no place to bring up a lady."

"Who wants to be a lady?" Peg retorted. "One of these days I might marry a red-headed lieutenant, have ten kids and send them all to the Point. Then you'll have to say 'sir' to your grandchildren."

"This I haven't mentioned yet," Delaney said softly, turning to St. Clair. "I'm savin' the worst 'til last, see. We've had no way before to make a contact with our man. Peg is goin' to be our contact. She's to be company for you, so anything you have to report, you can report through her."

St. Clair smiled at Peg Delaney. "That

could involve risk," he said. "If you know what I mean."

"I cut teeth on the stock of a Dragoon pistol," she said with a toss of her head. "Soldiers don't scare me, Mr. St. Clair. Not even a man who can whip Jim Overmile."

"Overmile?" St. Clair said, and looked around at the man he had whipped. His eyes swung back to Sergeant Delaney. "Is he with you, Sergeant?"

"Major Delafield said the lad he sent would be rash," Delaney said. "I was just findin' out."

CHAPTER 3

The next day a railroad ferry took them across the wide and muddy Mississippi River to St. Louis, and from there they traveled by Army ambulance and escort wagon to Jefferson Barracks. Sergeant Delaney and his daughter did not speak to St. Clair when they parted; to interested eyes they had been merely passengers on the same train with nothing in common save their destination.

St. Clair found himself with Jim Overmile. The man's face was mottled from St. Clair's drubbing and a large scab was forming on his lip. He was not much older than St. Clair but he showed the scars of many fights. Overmile lived by some wild code of his own and made no apology for it.

"We'll enlist and get assigned," Overmile said. "The sergeant will contact us later." He grinned and slapped St. Clair on the arm. "Be tellin' me the truth now, lad — was your mother really Irish?"

"As Paddy's pig. Her name was O'Harrahan."

"Faith now," Overmile said, "I love you like me own brother, God rest his soul."

"If you're going to be my nursemaid," St. Clair said, "we'd better not fight any more."

"It gets to be a habit when you've been in the Army as long as I have."

Overmile set the course for a long, squat building. St. Clair asked, "How did a muscle-bound Mick like you ever get important enough to be let in on this setup?"

The man's grin hurt his smashed lip but he didn't seem to mind. "I'll let you in on a secret, lad: I'm a Sergeant Major same as Delaney. Detached duty, you might say."

St. Clair shook his head. "Let's go ask the officer about an enlistment."

They took their places against the inner wall with a dozen other recruits and in due time were given a rough medical examination and sworn in. That afternoon they were lectured by a pink-cheeked second lieutenant, while another group of officers watched from the sidelines.

The roll was called and one officer, a dark-skinned man with a full mustache and goatee, indicated that he wanted St. Clair and Overmile. St. Clair nudged his new friend and Overmile spoke out of the side of his mouth.

43

"That's Buckley, lad. It's all right. It's supposed to work this way."

In the supply room they were issued their uniforms, carbines, bullet pouches, cap boxes, and bayonets which were little more than Bowie knives, being designed for digging latrine holes rather than fighting.

They carried all this to a long barracks and found spare bunks. The mattress ticks were filled with straw from the stable and then a sergeant came around and announced that he was in charge of 'you dumb sonsabitches.'

Sergeant Owen was tall and wire-thin, with a voice like a quartermaster mule-skinner. He wore his felt hat forward, the inner band riding just above his eyebrows.

As a supplement to his uniform, Sergeant Owen carried a heavy stick, and he flourished this occasionally as he talked.

Both St. Clair and Overmile knew about the 'club' in the army and what it was used for. Discipline in 1857 was a harsh force. Routine punishment could be twenty lashes while bucked to an escort wagon wheel, and an officer could have a trooper shot for insubordination during combat patrol.

"— An' I'm tellin' you bastards now,"

Owen was shouting, "if you got a god, then forget 'im, because I'm goin' to be your god in this re-croot detachment. I speak, an' you buggers better jump, but quick —"

He called attention and the recruits fell all over themselves trying to effect their own personal rendition. Sergeant Owen's stick whacked heads, knuckles, backsides. Then he spotted Overmile and St. Clair in immaculate positions and came over with a frown.

"What we got here?" he asked. "A couple o' goddam Prussian generals, that's what we got."

Across the trampled parade ground, other detachments were being shoved into shape, and near the troop barracks a sergeant detached himself and came over, smiling at Sergeant Owen's new brood.

"Well now," Sergeant Royce said softly, his eyes running up and down the double ranks. "That's a fine lot of scratch farmers and chicken thieves."

Sergeant Owen still stood before Troopers St. Clair and Overmile, his switch slapping nervously against his boot. The sergeant who had just spoken looked carefully at these two and said, "Old soldiers, Owen?"

"That's yet to be seen," Owen said. He

45

addressed them all: "Now see here, you slobs, I'm responsible for makin' troopers of you, and that's what I'll do or I'll break you doin' it, you understand?"

Their glum faces showed that they did and Sergeant Owen smiled. He took a peculiar satisfaction in the degrading of these men because he could recall so vividly his own life as a recruit, seven years before. Each new batch seemed to force his revulsion deeper, for in their awkward bungling he could see himself and he loathed the image.

With club and curse he drove them, some over the hill, others into the stockade, and the remainder into the immaculate pattern that is a soldier's prime asset: perfect discipline.

Sergeant Royce had the diamond of a top soldier inside the V of his hooks. Placing his hands on his hips, he let his eyes drift up and down the line, resting at last on St. Clair.

"My name is Sergeant Royce, and until I get an officer, I'm senior in E Troop. Where have you soldiered before? You speak up and you won't have to take this crap from Owen. I can use experienced men."

"I never said I'd soldiered," St. Clair said evenly.

46

Sergeant Royce frowned, an expression that came easily to him. He was a red-faced man with thick hair that protruded from under his cap. "Trooper, a recruit says 'sir' when he speaks to a non-commissioned officer. Now, I asked you a question. Don't I get an answer?"

Because Quincy St. Clair had endured nearly four years of merciless hazing and severe discipline, he found Sergeant Royce's overweening attitude almost laughable. "I'm afraid I've already been assigned," St. Clair said, "— sir."

"Now just a minute," Owen protested. "Dammit, every bunch of re-croots I get in, you got to come over and pick and choose. Maybe I ought to go to the commander about this."

Royce took Sergeant Owen by the shirt front and shook him once. "Maybe you'd get your head busted open in town some night too. You get paid for every man I can transfer. Now you watch these men, you hear? You know what I want."

"Sure," Owen mumbled, and turned to watch Sergeant Royce go back across the parade ground.

The bugler blew mess call and Owen dismissed his detachment, watching sourly as they turned to the mess at the end of the

47

barracks. Each outfit had its own eating quarters, a slab-sided enclosure at the end of the sleeping area. St. Clair drew Jim Overmile aside as the others filed in.

"You know what Royce was talking about?"

"Hell no," Overmile said. "Takin' recruits out of the detachment's old stuff. Commanders do it to keep their troops to full strength. Makes no difference if the man's trained or not; they'll do it in the field."

"You think that's it?"

Overmile shrugged. "Thinkin' ain't in my department. Let's chow up." He turned and went into the noisy mess-hall.

Even to experienced soldiers such as St. Clair and Overmile, there was a monotony to the recruit training that ground the mind numb. Each moment in their day was taken up by new processes, and when evening overtook them, they would eat and lie on their bunks.

St. Clair soon learned that Overmile was not all knuckles and hard head. Beneath the man's tough face lay a mind that moved with nimble speed. Lying in the bunk next to St. Clair, he sat up suddenly and jerked his head before going outside. St. Clair followed him a moment later.

Overmile had hunkered down against the barracks wall where darkness was ink. He said softly, "Sergeant Royce was snoopin' around again this morning. I heard some of the lads talkin', and I'm thinkin' he's lookin' for Southern gents."

"Where was I while this went on?" St. Clair asked.

"Spongin' dishes, darlin'," Overmile said. "Got any tobacco?"

St. Clair handed him a cigar and Overmile raked a match against the log wall. After he got it going he said, "Delaney was around but the scut gave no sign. I'm for gettin' out of here, bucko. I have no hankerin' for anymore of Owen or Royce."

"There's no 'out' until we're told to move out," St. Clair said. His cigar glowed and died and he shifted until he was sitting on the ground. "If you feel brave, talk up to Royce and see what he does."

"Not me, lad," Overmile said. "My job is to see that *you* don't step into somethin' that don't wipe off. Royce'll be around again in the mornin'. I'll leave it up to you."

Across the parade, the bugler blew tattoo. Overmile got up, following St. Clair into the rank-smelling barracks. Lamps

49

were being snuffed out and they settled on their bunks.

Gradually the post grew quiet until only the muted movement of the sentries marred the silence.

Trooper St. Clair did not get a chance to speak to Sergeant Royce. The man stayed away three days running. On the afternoon of the fourth day, Lieutenant Buckley rode onto the parade ground where the recruits were taking dismounted drill, and called St. Clair to one side.

"I'm Lieutenant Buckley," he said and smiled. His finger brushed his mustache. He was tall, lean-flanked, and his finely molded face bore the fashionable chin whiskers and sweeping mustaches that marked the cavalry officer. His eyes were kind as he spoke. "Sorry about this, St. Clair, but we must at least pretend to go through channels."

"I quite understand, sir," St. Clair said.

"Report to C Troop orderly room in fifteen minutes," Buckley said quietly. It was his habit to speak softly and men inured to the usual shout found themselves straining to capture his words. His bearing and manner commanded attention. "You'll find it across the parade near headquarters."

He mounted up and rode away and St.

Clair returned to the barracks. He found Jim Overmile packing. "Delaney was over, me lad," he said. "I'll move the gear."

"I'll meet you in the troop barracks," St. Clair said, and went outside. Sergeant Owen had turned the marching recruits over to a corporal and was now by the mess-hall door, talking to Sergeant Royce.

When they saw St. Clair exit from the barracks, they moved along a path that intercepted him against the edge of the parade. "Well, now, you've not stayed long," Sergeant Royce said. He rocked back on his heels, his head tipped a little as he studied St. Clair from beneath his drooping hat brim. "You sure you don't want to join a real troop? I've got my bunch whipped into some real Jim Dandys." He spoke to Owen without taking his eyes from St. Clair. "Go find yourself a recruit to chew."

Owen resented the tone but he turned away and walked back to his own detachment. "What's on your mind, Sergeant?" St. Clair asked.

"Now is something on my mind?" Royce grinned. "Been hearin' some quiet talk about you, St. Clair. The word's around that you got into some trouble at the Academy. A real rebel who liked to raise

51

hell once too often. Personally, I never liked rules myself."

"What I did is my business."

"Sure, sure." Royce's manner was friendly. "I know about such things, St. Clair; sure I do. Lot of silly damned rules to bother a man when he doesn't intend a speck of harm. Surprises me that you'd sign up. I mean — what do you owe 'em anyway?"

Keep talking, mister.

"What else is there?" St. Clair said. "You train to be a soldier, then end up with the rug pulled out from under you. My father would have thrown me out of the house."

"I understand," Royce said softly. "You should have come into my troop. The men there'd understand same's I do. You get in another outfit and they'll treat you like you got the mumps. You ought to smarten up, St. Clair."

"If it gets tough, I'll transfer," St. Clair said.

"Be too late then," Royce pointed out. "Officers think only of buildin' their troops to strength. Now in E Troop, we got some bucko lads who'd like you. You can still change your mind. Say the word and I'll fix it up for you."

"How? You're not an officer."

"Maybe I'm not," Royce said, grinning, "but I got officers eatin' out of my hand. Don't you forget that."

"I'll remember," St. Clair told him, and walked on across the parade ground. Entering C Troop orderly room, he was admitted to Lieutenant Buckley's room by a corporal. Buckley shut the door and offered his hand and a smile.

"Damned glad to see you," he said, and waved St. Clair into a chair. Buckley offered a cigar and a light and when their smokes were drawing he said, "I didn't want to leave you in the recruit detachment any longer than necessary, but I wanted you to stay long enough for Owen and Royce to spot you for an old soldier. Now that I've pulled you into the troop, they'll think it's because I'm eager to pad my ranks, which I am."

"The post seems drastically under strength," St. Clair said, puffing gently to taste the flavor of his cigar.

Lieutenant Buckley smiled. "Less than half strength is closer to the truth. I have four troops of cavalry here and three officers to command them. B Troop, under Lieutenant McAuliff, has thirty-one men, almost one third strength. I have a little over forty, slightly less than half. D Troop

53

is commanded by Lieutenant Chambers. Sergent Royce commands E until we can get an officer to replace him. I'm short officers, men and equipment and there seems to be no relief in sight."

He paused to kick ash from his cigar with his little finger. "Captain Ackerman, who is commanding the Second, has gone on to Fort Riley to line up enough replacements to fill our ranks. We'll be moving out in a week, maybe less. Then the fun will begin." He scrubbed a hand across his cheek and paced about the room, streamers of cigar smoke eddying around his head and shoulders. Buckley was no more than thirty but he wore an older man's seriousness.

"This seems to be the logical place to build up the troop strength," St. Clair said.

Buckley nodded. "I've tried. Ackerman's driven himself crazy trying. But there's been no success. Every attempt we've made has been filed or shelved or blocked in some manner." He turned to face St. Clair. "I have to make a thirty-five day march across hostile country with a hundred and forty-odd men."

"Do you suspect that this — uncooperative attitude is deliberate?"

"Yes," Buckley said. "The Army is a

mess right now — split right down the middle. One of these days they'll line us all up on the parade and let the Southern boys go home. Kansas and Missouri are hotbeds, neighbor shooting at neighbor. It's getting so a man can't trust himself."

Buckley sat down behind his rough pine desk and leaned his forearms on it. "St. Clair, I'm not worried too much about the men who go around whistling 'Dixie.' I know, generally speaking, who's in sympathy with the Southern cause and who isn't. It's the ones I don't know who keep me awake at night."

"Sergeant Royce, sir?"

"Perhaps," Buckley said, and studied the tip of his cigar. "Royce seems to talk a great deal, but I feel there's more to the man than appears on the surface."

"He approached me about changing to E Troop," St. Clair said. "He's a careful man with his words, sir, and he's smarter than he lets on. I got the impression that he could override your orders if he had to — that he had connections higher up." St. Clair paused for a moment. "I don't presume to advise sir, but I consider it risky to allow Sergeant Royce to continue in a command capacity."

"I've thought of it," Buckley said. "Suppose I took him out and put someone else in his place? If he has any connections, then I might find myself relieved to a point where my primary function would be restricted. I'm interested primarily in just who are the minds who are pushing this upheaval within the Army ranks." He stood up and crossed to a wall map. "It took Western Union nine weeks to string a hundred miles of wire through here. Why? Because everything under the sun went wrong. Mules were stolen. There were shipping delays from the East. The Indians raised hell." He rolled the map and tossed it on his desk. "We're bucking a well organized Copperhead force and it will take some dangerous digging to uncover the top men."

"Exactly where do I fit in?"

"I think you're already fitting in," Buckley said. "Royce got wind of your 'desertion' and has tried to get you in E Troop. That could mean something, or nothing. I keep the sergeant close where I can watch and control him. When and if he steps over the line, I'll have him shot."

Buckley glanced at the sour stub of his cigar and shied it into the coal scuttle. "There isn't much you can do around here, except watch Royce and see what you can learn. He's our prime suspect so far. You're going to get in your licks when we get to the Smoky Hill River country where the real trouble is. I'll make a runner of you; that will allow you to move around almost at will. Somewhere along the line someone will make a slip and I trust you'll be sharp enough to catch it."

"Should an event arise that calls for immediate action," St. Clair said, "how far can I go, sir?"

"You've been trained as an officer for the United States Army," Buckley said, "but you may not do anything that might reveal that fact. I've studied your record, St. Clair, and I want to warn you that in my troop I prefer a steady, capable man who lives by the book — a thing you apparently don't do too well. I assure you I want no heroes. Just give me efficiency without any glory hunting, understand?"

St. Clair flushed and nodded.

"Tonight, I want you to go into Crystal City. The town is a hotbed and there are men there who do nothing but watch our movements. Overmile has orders to pull you into a party that's going, but I want it clearly understood that you're there to observe, not to embroil yourself in any trouble that might arise."

"I understand, sir," St. Clair said. He stood up.

Buckley offered his hand again. "Some day we'll sit down at the officers' mess and have a good laugh over this. In the meantime, good luck, and be damned careful."

"That sounds ominous," St. Clair said. "I heard that two officers were killed trying to do what I'm about to try."

"Yes," Buckley admitted. "Remember, the men you're fighting need no proof. Just a sneaking suspicion, and they'll get you. And by the same token, neither do you need it. If you believe that an officer or enlisted man is acting beyond the capacity of his position, report it to Sergeant Delaney or his daughter. I will act on your judgment and leave the conclusions up to you. In such a case you'll be judge and jury."

"Yes, sir," St. Clair said. He went down the duckboards to C Troop barracks.

Overmile had put away St. Clair's gear and he hailed him as soon as St. Clair appeared. "Laddie Buck, 'tis old friends I'm makin' here." He waved his hand at two troopers sitting near the far end. "I've been thinkin'," he said, coming up to St. Clair and putting an arm around his shoulder, "that a night in town would do us a world of good. There's fun to be had, lad — a fight, a woman's kiss. That's all there is for a soldier, besides soldierin'."

He laughed loudly and went down the aisle toward his two friends. "Joe, Willie, get out the foo-foo powder. Friend Quincy has th' money for all of us."

St. Clair put on his forager cap and yellow lined cape, joining Overmile and his two friends outside. Willie Carp was the humorous one while Joe Axton was merely a sober man in need of a drink.

In front of regimental headquarters they waited for an escort wagon to take them to town. St. Clair leaned against the building and listened to their talk. A dozen men were gathered here, all bent toward one destination. Surprisingly, he did not feel alien to these men, their attitudes, the processes of their thinking.

And I should, he thought. As an officer I should be different.

From a lifetime of training, Quincy St. Clair had always thought of an officer's role as being slightly gallant. He could recall with ease the magnificence of marching cadets on the Plain above the Hudson, the lilt of the regimental band, the guidons flying, sabers flashing in the sunlight.

A trooper never sees that, he mused uncomfortably. *A trooper only sees the manure piles and the hundred other obnoxious details.*

The escort wagon arrived and the troopers piled in, through the back, over the sides, shoving for a place to sit, and then the driver cracked the whip and moved out.

Sergeant Royce saw to it that each of the men with him had a drink in his hand and his interest firmly held by the talk at the bar before he left them to saunter down the street. He paused at the corner, then veered right where the night was thick and the traffic thin. At the alley he paused again to listen, then navigated its gloomy length and emerged on the edge of town where a narrow-gauge railroad made twin metallic streaks in the thin moonlight. There was an equipment shed to one side and beyond that a telegrapher's shack.

Sergeant Royce rapped on the door, which opened immediately.

The telegrapher was a balding man, nervous and somewhat irritable. He handed Royce a telegram. "This came in over an hour ago. Them fellas better be careful on the other end. The day operator hadn't been gone ten minutes. Was he to find out, there'd be trouble."

Royce read the message and cursed.

Opening the door of the pot-bellied stove, he tossed it in. He watched the flames consume it, then toed the door shut. "So St. Clair is a Yankee officer?"

"What you goin' to do?" The telegrapher took him by the sleeve. "Now don't go gettin' me in trouble. I got a wife an' four kids to feed."

"You keep punchin' your little key," Royce advised, and went back to the saloon. He paused at the bar long enough to see that his men had whiskey left in the bottle, then went up the stairs to the second floor.

The hall was illuminated by only one lamp and he walked through this half darkness to the end and tapped softly on a door. A voice on the other side said, "Who is it?"

"Royce."

The bolt slid back and Royce stepped inside. "I came from the telegraph office," Royce said, and sat down. A lamp burned on the desk but the shade threw the light downward, leaving the upper half of the room in darkness. The man sat down behind his desk. He was heavy through the shoulders and his face was moon-shaped with side whiskers and a thick mustache. "The Army's sent another spy," Royce went on. "Clever this time. They took a Point man just before graduation and dummied up a desertion charge."

"Better send a wire to Fort Riley," the big man said.

"I can handle this," Royce said. "I'll need your help, Ranier. This has to look good."

"It always does," the big man said. He tilted back in his chair. "What are you going to do about Buckley?"

"Nothing, right now," Royce said flatly. "Once I kill off his boy, he can only cuss and ask for another." He stood up and moved to the door. "I'll see what I can do to set him up for you. Stay awake for your chance."

"Sure," Ranier said, and Sergeant Royce stepped out and down the stairs to the bar room.

The Army escort wagon pulled to a stop before the broad hotel steps and the soldiers dismounted. The driver called, "Leaves at one sharp, although I doubt you'll be sober enough to find it."

"Gettin' drunk's a trooper's solemn duty," Overmile told him, and then glanced around, scanning the traffic like a dog seeking a scent.

Crystal City was a sprawling little town on the west bank of the Mississippi, Southern to the core, but not so patriotic that it couldn't dedicate itself to a trooper's pleasure. After sundown, the residential district to the south barred its doors and entertained in the parlor, while on Main Street dirty-shirt blue flowed up and down and the sharp, squealing laughter of women blared from the town's twelve saloons.

The largest of these were located on the four corners of the town square. The upstairs windows were heavily curtained and masked a brisk trade that continued until early morning.

"I know of a place —" Willie Carp began.

"Any damn place," Joe Axton said. "I've got a hell of a thirst, I have."

The doors winnowed in the saloon across the street and two men came out to stand on the porch. In the dim light spilling past, St. Clair made out Sergeant Royce and a big man. He nudged Jim Overmile who grunted and said, "Yeah." In a louder voice he added, "Well, across then, me buckos."

Royce turned back and went inside. The big man was still standing there when the four men from C Troop filed past. His eyes were bright buttons over his cigar.

Inside the saloon the din was almost deafening as troopers shifted about, seemingly without aim, gambling, drinking, laughing uproariously, as if this was their last night on earth and they were determined to enjoy it.

A dozen girls cruised the floor, their brief costumes revealing shapely calves and bare shoulders. In one corner a five-piece band strained to be heard above the confusion. A fight broke out and two burly bouncers quickly squelched it.

At the bar, Overmile bullied a place for them and pounded for the sweating bartender's attention. Served at last, he tossed off his drink and jerked a thumb toward St. Clair. "My friend here will pay," he said, and St. Clair laid a dollar on the bar.

St. Clair swiveled around and hooked his elbows on the bar to watch the crowd. Royce and six of his men were clustered around a poker table, trying to take a dandied gambler's money.

Overmile edged close to St. Clair and said, "Royce has his boys with him. You got any ideas, better forget 'em. Buckley don't want trouble."

"You worry too much," St. Clair said

softly. "I'm going to take a look around. Stay here until I get back."

Once out of the saloon, the noise abated and seemed to come from some far-off place. On the street corners, barkers hawked the games and tried to entice trade inside. Along one side street soldiers wandered back and forth through the darkness, coming and going, talking and laughing. Leaning against a corner post of the hotel arcade, St. Clair watched them, noticing that they hurried off as though pushed by an unseen hand, but when they returned they walked easy and free, as though the darkness had rinsed away some troubling frustration. Of the two sides to this town, apparently only the bad was offered the troopers.

From the doorway of the hotel he heard a familiar voice and turned. Peg Delaney came to the edge of the porch where he stood. Her eyes were amused as she said, "You look good in dirty-shirt blue."

He swept off his forager cap and stood tall and straight, smiling faintly. "This town's no place for you. Another hour and it'll be wild."

"The troopers?" She shook her head. "I understand them. Nothing would happen to me." Her eyebrow rose a little. "But

65

something might happen to you. Did you have to come in?"

"Orders," he said. "You're Army. You know what orders are."

"And sometimes I don't like to take them."

"That's what sets the thirty-year professional apart," he said, "the ability to take any kind of order." He stopped talking when a soldier stumbled against the boardwalk and nearly fell at St. Clair's feet. The soldier got up and lurched against St. Clair who gave him a shove that sent him tumbling backward.

The soldier caught himself and faced St. Clair. "You want trouble?" He waited, half drunk and full of fight.

"Baker!" Peg Delaney snapped. "Mind your manners when I'm talking to someone!"

"Sorry, ma'am," the soldier mumbled, and lurched across the street. He paused on the other side and looked at St. Clair as though firmly implanting the image of the tall man in his mind. Then Baker went into the saloon.

St. Clair did not stop to analyze his sudden anger. He felt it build up and let it go. "Don't ever do that to me again!"

"You're very proud," Peg said, that tantalizing smile near the surface of her eyes. "Habit is strong in you, St. Clair. You were on the verge of calling him to attention and dressing him down. Or, perhaps you would have caught yourself in time and decided to fight him. You wouldn't have had an easy time of it, though. Baker's a rough one. He's also Royce's man."

St. Clair's voice was brittle with control. "I don't know what standing orders you have, but in the future keep your nose out of affairs that are mine."

She was suddenly angry. "You *are* a martinet, aren't you? I pity the woman who becomes your wife. You'll probably insist that she speak to you from the position of attention."

He wanted to hurt her then, to crush her with words, to get even. *Even for what?* Because he had no answer his anger melted away. He glanced past her as her father came from the hotel to the porch edge.

He glanced from his daughter to St. Clair and said, "I see you're fightin' already. Should have warned you, Quincy — she's a Kilkenny cat when she gets her ear up."

"We were having a simple discussion," Peg said. She refused to look at her father or St. Clair.

67

Sergeant Delaney smiled to himself and then asked, "Overmile across the street?" St. Clair nodded. "Best stay out of there then. Overmile's a good man in a tight one and he can take care of himself." He stepped from the porch, then paused. "That man you pushed was Baker and chances are that he wasn't as drunk as he seemed. Baker's from Tennessee and he likes a knife."

With that off his mind, Delaney walked on down the street to a small saloon that was the haunt of noncoms. Peg stirred and St. Clair saw that she was still angry.

He stepped close enough to touch her and stood there, his forager cap in his hands. "Peg, I'm sorry. I was wrong picking on you that way."

"You meant it," she said. "You wanted to hurt me, didn't you? Well, you did. Was it because of your girl?"

"I don't know," he admitted. "Whatever it was, I'm truly sorry."

"Don't be," she said quickly, then laughed. "I have a devil of a temper. Would you like to walk with me? You understand that I am an enlisted man's daughter and therefore it's improper for an officer to — but then you *are* an enlisted man, at least temporarily."

"You're dealing in technicalities," he said and took her arm. St. Clair threaded their way through the crowd without obvious effort. He allowed no one to brush against her, yet he never seemed to move out of his way to do this. Turning west on a quiet side street, they walked for three blocks.

Peg Delaney said, "This must be the proper part of town."

"Well, we're proper people," he told her. The boardwalk was ink beneath the tall oaks.

She walked in silence for a moment, the tap of her heels matching his. "Who did you really want to hurt back there? Me? Or just any woman?"

"Guessing is fun but you can get a lot of wrong answers that way."

"Not this time," she said. "Quincy, you're a smart man, a controlled man; but that wasn't what we were talking about, was it? I imagine you were terribly noble with her — the girl back in Highland Falls. Hand kissing, and polite conversation." She shot him a sidelong look. "You don't have to tell me about her if you don't want to."

"That's nice to know." He was smiling.

"But then if you don't, I'll wonder, and after a while you'll wonder what I'm won-

69

dering — is that terribly complicated? So it would be easier all around if you'd tell me, wouldn't it?" She laughed softly. "I think a general might call that strategy."

"You're a hussy."

"No news to you," she said.

"There's the courthouse square over there." He pointed. "Care to sit?"

"I think it would be safe," she said hesitantly. "Were you wearing your bars, I'd plead a headache and go back to the hotel, but with a trooper I'm always safe."

"I'm not really a trooper," he said, "and I don't follow that." He saw that she was seated and spread his cape on the ground before her.

"Suppose you were openly an officer instead of an enlisted man," she said. "You'd have some bargaining points, and when a man has those he always bargains, even when he doesn't mean it. An officer makes enough money to marry and his future is more secure than a trooper's. Some would say his social life is superior."

"Ouch," St. Clair said. "I didn't think I was that obvious."

"To most people you aren't, but a woman notices things. Tell me about the girl."

"You're like the railroad at the edge of

town," he said. "You go so far, then stop." She was, he decided, pert, snoopy and self-willed, but strikingly honest, and he found that he liked her more than any girl he had ever known. She said things to him that would have been unpardonable from another woman, but he accepted them even when they pinched.

"The soldier's strongest point is his tenacity." She touched his hand. Here the wild sounds of the other street seemed far removed. "You really don't have to tell me, but I'm dying to hear."

"She's very pretty," St. Clair said, "and I *did* tell her that I loved her. But I don't think she took me seriously. Perhaps you're right about that bargaining business. I had graduation ahead, and a commission. The easy things."

"Do you really want to marry her, or was it just a whim to be engaged?"

"That's not easy to answer," he admitted.

"Never mind," Peg said. "My imagination can supply the rest."

"Devil take your imagination," he said. "It's far too lively as it is."

She laughed at him, but she could laugh in such a way that it didn't bother him. "I'm just a dull Army brat, always on the outside looking in. When Dad retires I'll forget my good sense and marry an officer. That would be permissible providing he was out of the service."

"Now who's sour on the subject."

"I am," she admitted. "Living on Suds Row is no fun." She stood up and offered her hand. "We'd better be getting back. I imagine Jim Overmile's bottle is about empty."

He put on his cape and forager cap. "You're so smart; what brand?"

She placed a finger against her cheek. "Let's see now. You paid for it, but Jim's drinking habits are pretty well established. I'd say Joe Gideon barrel whiskey. You could afford better but habit would make him order it."

"Truly an amazing deduction," St. Clair said. "Peg, I've never met anyone like you. I mean that."

"We'd really better go," she said. "After thinking about it I'm only half safe with you. Pretending to be a trooper is still only pretending."

"Peg —" he began, but she placed a palm against his chest.

"Don't. See? You have an officer's mind and you think you *have* to say something sweet to me. Don't, Quincy. You have one girl and that's enough for any man."

"I don't know that I have a girl any more," he said. "Damn it, Peg, you don't let a man finish."

"Someday, I'll let the right man finish," she told him. "I'm not like some women, Quincy. It doesn't flatter me when a man says something that makes a fool of him."

CHAPTER 4

Sergeant Delaney was waiting on the hotel porch when they returned. Peg went inside and St. Clair stood by the sergeant, watching the soldier traffic stream up and down the street. Their boots scuffed the dust until it hung like a fog between the slab-sided buildings.

Delaney said, "Hatchet's buried, I see."

"She's an extraordinary girl," St. Clair admitted, and that drew the sergeant's smile.

"Army clean through," he said proudly. "First toys she had was a Comanche rattle made from buff'lo toes and a stuffed rag of an Army blanket for a doll. Seemed to satisfy her though." He jerked his thumb toward the saloon across the street. "Overmile's not come out yet, and the bottle's about empty."

"They still on their feet?"

"If a bottle of whiskey knocked one of my troopers off his feet, I'd transfer him in the marnin'. There may be a fight in the makin', but I'd stay out of it if I was you.

74

Baker's come to the door half a dozen times."

St. Clair's eyes brightened and a rash wind rocked him. A part of his mind told him to forget it, but still another urged action. "Looking for me, you think?"

"I'd say so. Somethin's in the wind and the only way to find out what, is to go over there. That's what they want."

"And that's my intention," St. Clair said. He walked across the street, ignoring Delaney's warning shout that followed him. He paused at the swinging doors and looked over them. Baker was moving in his direction but stopped, as he spotted St. Clair. The man wheeled abruptly and went back to Sergeant Royce and the other men of E Troop.

St. Clair pushed the batwings aside and walked to the bar to join Jim Overmile, Axton and Carp. Royce and his men were near the far end.

One of the bartenders edged along the cherrywood and said, "Royce, let's have a quiet time of it now or take it outside."

"Shut up," Sergeant Royce said flatly. He gave his attention to St. Clair. "You been gone so long I about gave you up. Baker here tells me you're real tough."

"Please!" the bartender wailed, then

threw his towel aside and ran for the stairs. "Mr. Ranier!"

A soldier standing against the wall stepped out to block him. "Easy there, Shorty. They just want to have a round or two."

"They'll wreck the place!" the bartender complained. He looked wide-eyed as Sergeant Royce rolled his shoulders and stepped clear of the bar. The men with Royce fanned out and quickly cut off Overmile, Axton and Carp by engaging them. St. Clair realized then that this was coming off very smoothly for Royce.

No one but Royce moved and he kept closing in on St. Clair. The others waited, ready to jump Overmile and the other two when Royce gave some signal. Acting as if he were going to offer no fight, St. Clair lashed out as Royce closed in, catching the sergeant on the bridge of the nose.

Then St. Clair whirled away.

The stinging power of the blow halted Royce. He stood there, shocked, then wildly angry when the blood started to dribble. Overmile divined Royce's purpose and bounded into two men while Axton and Carp piled into the others. Axton sledged one man, driving him halfway across the room into a poker table, then went down as a trooper belted him across the back with a chair.

Coming around now with a full head of rage, Royce swung at St. Clair, who danced away and whirled to strike another trooper who was crowding Overmile. He kept away from Royce, making the sergeant come to him. When Royce did, St. Clair cut him with flicking fists before retreating.

Carp and a trooper were battering each other. Then the trooper went skidding across the floor and Carp followed in a long dive that missed and left him sprawled. Moving again toward Royce, St. Clair boxed with the man, a method of fighting Royce did not understand. St. Clair hit him in the stomach, then kept him off balance. Royce landed several cutting blows but St. Clair caught the sergeant against the bar and snapped his head back with an axing right.

Behind him, Overmile had released one of the troopers and had another by the collar and seat of the pants, ramming him headfirst into the bar. The man's head made a hollow booming against the cherrywood.

Royce was weak and badly hurt and St. Clair decided that this was the time to get out of the fight. He had a bleeding cut over one eye and his head throbbed from a dozen blows. From a far corner Carp shouted, "Look out for the bouncers!"

Four men were thumping down the stairs, all armed with sawed-off billiard cues. St. Clair slammed Royce a crippling blow, then backed away and edged toward the door. Carp and Axton broke away from the fight, as did Overmile, but the bouncers came on. St. Clair noticed that one man's cue was thicker than the rest and somewhat longer.

As though by prearrangement, Royce and E Troop faded to the far side of the room. The bouncers did not give them a second glance. They converged on St. Clair and his friends and then St. Clair realized what was so odd about the one bouncer's stick.

It was not a stick at all but a single-barreled shotgun with only a pistol grip for a stock. "Look out!" he yelled, and dived for the shelter of an up-ended table as the room bulged with sound.

The charge of double 0 buckshot gnawed a slice from the oak rim. St. Clair tore at the buttons of his tunic, trying to get at the .36 Navy Colt tucked in his waistband. Men were yelling and he recognized Carp's highpitched bleat.

"Get that man with the gun! He's reloading!"

Overmile and Axton had closed with two of the bouncers and the third stalked Carp. Thrusting his head around the table, St. Clair saw the bouncer with the shotgun slip a brass percussion cap on the nipple and bring the hammer to full cock. The bouncer whipped the shotgun into line and St. Clair fired, the report of the .36 a sharp crack above the roar of fighting men.

The bouncer staggered back a step and tried to raise his gun. Thumbing back the hammer, St. Clair planted another ball squarely in the man's breastbone. The bouncer turned and fell, the shotgun discharging into the ceiling. The room reeked with the odor of black powder.

As quickly as it had started, the fight ended. Royce and his men were moving toward a rear door and the three bouncers left Overmile and Axton, rushing to their fallen comrade. St. Clair left the shelter of the table as Sergeant Delaney spilled through the doorway, a huge .44 Dragoon Colt in his fist.

His eyes took in what had happened and he said, "Outside!" His huge arms propelled Overmile, Axton and Carp toward the door. On the porch he said, "Get out of town fast, Overmile. Take the men with you."

Someone was shouting inside the saloon and Delaney pushed St. Clair ahead of him, hurrying him along the walk. At a cross street they stopped and stood just around the corner where the night was thickest.

"Quincy, my boy, that was supposed to have been a murder in there," Delaney said. He blew out a ragged breath and peeked around the corner. Several civilians emerged from the saloon and looked up and down the street. There was a lot of shouting. "I think you killed him," Delaney added. "That was Rance Ranier, a big man in these parts."

"You ever had anyone pepper you with a shotgun?" St. Clair asked. He tucked his pistol back in his waistband and pulled his tunic over it.

"We'll do well to get back to the post," Delaney said. He went ahead of St. Clair down the side street, talking softly as he walked. "They didn't know you were armed. Ranier could have said afterward that someone joggled his arm durin' the fight and it was so sad you'd been killed. I have no doubt now that's the way it was planned."

"Royce was in on it," St. Clair said flatly. "He sure stepped out of Ranier's way when he came downstairs with his three playmates."

"We'll watch Royce close from now on," Delaney said. He made a circuit around the center of the town, going down one alley after another. Finally they came to an Army ambulance and Delaney motioned for St. Clair to get in the back.

"But how did they single me out?" he asked. "Royce must have pointed to me earlier in the evening. They had me pinpointed before the fight started."

"Probably," Delaney agreed. He clucked to the team. "Stay down in the back now. We'll worry out the details in Lieutenant Buckley's office. He'll not be pleased, I'm thinkin'."

As they rattled out of town, St. Clair felt the tightness leave his nerves. He began to breathe easier, and then Peg Delaney spoke up from the seat. "An exciting night, wasn't it, Quincy?" She had been leaning against the dark corner and her presence startled him.

"Depends on what you like in the way of excitement," St. Clair said. Then he pillowed his aching head in his arms and braced himself against the rock and sway of the ambulance.

★ ★ ★

Some will stoutly maintain that New York State is more beautiful in the spring when the trees and flowers burst into bloom, than in the fall when the oaks and maples flash their burnished leaves before spilling them to the ground.

But Lieutenant Niles Upton was in no mood to compare the wonders of nature. With the ceremony over and his gold braid shoulder boxes sewn into place, Lieutenant Upton contemplated his orders and wondered what he had done to deserve such an assignment.

His mother, who had come up from Norfolk to see him graduate, soon lost interest in manly affairs and joined a lady from Portsmouth with whom she was acquainted, leaving Lieutenant Upton alone to ponder his future.

Taking a seat beneath an old oak, Upton waited patiently until Alex Howison came over and sat down beside him. "Congratulations, Lieutenant," Howison said, smiling slightly. "You're a fine looking officer, Niles."

"Fine be damned," Upton said. "You promised me a Washington post and I've been ordered to the frontier."

"Our plans have been changed," Howison

said, and licked a cigar before lighting it. "St. Clair is dead by now. In a few days Major Delafield will be notified and the brass will put their heads together. I imagine it will be quite a blow because St. Clair was good for the job. He represented their last-ditch effort."

"Then why must I —"

"To take charge when the time comes," Howison said. "I need a man to replace Royce, Niles. He's all right for the rough work but I need a man who can command. We're going to do more than these isolated harassing forays." He leaned forward to tap Upton on the knee with his finger. "Niles, Western Union is still moving along too fast. They are surmounting these, ah — obstacles. Lieutenant Buckley has been ordered to the Smoky Hill with four troops. I've done all in my power to keep him from gaining full strength, but when he reaches Fort Riley he'll be reenforced there. You can serve us best in Buckley's command."

Howison stood up and smiled at Upton. "There's an officer at Fort Riley who'll know you and will make a contact. I envy you, Niles — your youth, the golden opportunities ahead of you. A magnificent future. It wouldn't surprise me if you became a general in the Southern army. Maybe

83

even a governor." He sighed and shifted his cigar from one corner of his mouth to the other. "I'm a very ambitious man, Niles. I like power. But unlike you, I don't have the blood of Southern aristocracy flowing through my veins. I'm content to create a general or a governor, then sit back and enjoy the well-earned profits. You've been taught how to be a Yankee in outward appearance. Do a good job for us, Niles. We're counting on you."

He turned and walked away.

But still another man wished an audience with the new lieutenant — a small, rather nondescript man. Seeing Upton alone now, he crossed the lawn and removed his hat.

"Lieutenant Upton? I don't believe I've had the pleasure of meeting you. Shall we talk?"

Upton looked the man over. Who was he, some boot salesman?

"I'm sure you'll thank me for seeing you in private like this," the man added. "As soon as you sense the delicacy of the matter."

"Very well," Upton agreed. He walked with the man to a grove of trees. "Now what the deuce do you want?"

"A talk about your future," the man said.

"I'm Glorianna's father and I take it you're going to marry her without any fuss."

"Marry?" *The man must be insane!* "I'm afraid your daughter has misinformed you, sir. I never promised to marry her."

"I'm not interested in what went between you two in the way of talk," Mr. Holland said. He looked at Upton with wise eyes. He had a habit of talking with quick darting gestures of his hands. "She's due to show her condition in a little while. There isn't anything a person can do to hide a thing like that, you know."

What was the man saying? Upton began to strangle. "You don't think that I —" He tried a gusty, snorting laugh and nearly choked.

"No need to get upset," Mr. Holland said calmly. "Man gets his finger cut off in a saw, he don't stop to worry about which tooth did it. Now she's pointed to you and I'm going to see that you do the right thing."

"This is impossible! What you suggest is out of the question!"

"Let's look at it another way," Holland suggested. "I could take a shotgun and make you marry her, but I don't own a shotgun. Then again, you could get hostile and refuse. I guess it would make her sad, but there wouldn't be much she could do, except let folks know who the father was. It appears to me that the government takes a dim view of its officers getting into this kind of trouble. Could cost a man his commission, couldn't it?"

"I need time to think," Upton said weakly.

"What's there to think about?" Holland wanted to know. He put a hand on Upton's shoulder. "Don't take it so hard, *son*. She's a bit flighty but still a good eyeful. With the right husband, she'll do fine."

Upton leaned against a tree for support, a fine film of sweat making a shine on his face. He made vague motions with his hands. "What can I say? I'm innocent. I'm — I'm an officer and a gentleman! Surely you see the impossibility of this."

Holland chuckled. "Lieutenant, I've lived longer than you. When a man's a rooster, the gentleman in him don't make him a damn bit different from a barnyard chicken."

"Really, now —"

"I expect we'd best have a quiet wedding. I'll take care of the details."

"I refuse! Absolutely refuse!"

Holland sighed. "Writing to the adjutant-general won't be easy —"

Upton seized him by the collar and pulled him close. "Now, now," Holland cautioned. "I'm not very big but I can yell loud. What I'll yell will sound pretty bad."

Upton released the man. "Very well. How long do I have?"

"Tomorrow's soon enough. Come to the house at ten in the morning. I wouldn't be late if I was you."

Lieutenant Upton watched Holland waddle across the lawn. Then Alex Howison detached himself from a group and came over.

"What did he want?"

In terse phrases, Niles Upton covered the bulk of Holland's terms. Alex Howison swore under his breath. "You blundering fool," Howison said.

"I swear to God I had nothing to do with this," Upton said. He paused as a new thought struck him. "St. Clair! This is his doing!" He took Howison by the sleeve and shook him. "Don't you see?"

"I see that you've lost your wits," Howison said. "St. Clair was ordered to leave the post, to desert. I was instrumental in selecting him for the job, just as I was instrumental in selecting you to give him an excuse for deserting."

"But — I thought he was killed — I

mean, I had no idea this was all a plan."

Howison's voice grew hard. "You are not getting paid to think. I'll do the thinking and if you follow orders everything will come out the way I want it. Now marry that girl! That's an order! I can't afford to have a private stink ruin my plans."

Alex Howison calmed himself and bit the end from a fresh cigar. "Listen to me, Niles. I don't take chances. I make a plan and I stick to it and I'm not in the habit of explaining myself to my subordinates. However, since the situation now involves a personal matter, I'll break my own rule. Holland is a merchant and like most of us he's ambitious. I advanced him a considerable sum of money and I have a great deal of control over him."

"Then you could get me out of —"

"I'll get you out of nothing," Howison said flatly. "Niles, it was my original intention to embroil St. Clair in personal difficulties in order to eliminate him when Major Delafield and Wade Garland first mentioned him as a potential agent. I'd disposed of two officers already and I didn't feel that I should risk a third. It was then that I learned of your midnight trysts with Glorianna Holland." Howison spread his hands. "You can see what a position I found myself in. To expose St. Clair was to expose you, something I couldn't afford to do. I'm sorry, Niles, but this will have to work out for the best. Marriage gives a young officer respectability. You'll need it."

Upton groaned, despising the web in which he found himself entangled. Howison smiled around his cigar and slapped him on the arm before walking away.

Upton sat down beneath the tree and contemplated a bleak future.

He spent the rest of the day and evening in a fog, talking, yet not remembering what he said. The morning dawned cold and windy and he went reluctantly to the Holland home where a quiet ceremony was performed. Afterward the family accompanied them to the depot. No one spoke at the station. Upton's mother wept a little, overwhelmed by the suddenness of the marriage. Glorianna's father kissed her briefly, then climbed in his buggy and drove away without a backward glance, clearly relieved to be rid of this worry.

Glorianna refrained from tears, breaking her whitefaced silence only to say, "I'm sorry, Niles, but I had to do it."

"Did you really?" His voice was a winter wind.

"I'll make it up to you," she promised.

"Really?" He held his head erect and looked at her with such scorn that she recoiled and waited in silence. His mother, realizing through her bewilderment that she was not wanted here, turned away and got into her carriage.

Lieutenant Upton remained stonily silent.

Highland Falls was quiet at this hour. The shaded trees, the lingering scent of night blooming jasmine, the soft voices of birds, combined to make this an enchanted spot.

To Lieutenant Upton the whole affair resembled a nightmare from which he held no hope of waking.

I'm chained to her now, he thought. *Divorce is impossible for an officer. She'll never die. Her kind lives forever. . . .*

He tried to turn his thoughts to the future and the job he had to do, but because he was driven by ambition and not patriotism, he could find little comfort there.

Lieutenant Jules Buckley's anger charged the room with tension. Sergeant Delaney sat with his chair tipped back against the wall of Buckley's office, doing his best to remain neutral. Quincy St. Clair had dismantled his .36 Navy Colt's pistol and cleaned the bore. Now he reassembled the barrel and frame, crushed two paper cartridges with the rammer, and capped the two bare nipples.

Buckley sat behind his desk, his fingers laced tightly together. The lamp puddled light on the desk and left the rest of the small room in semi-darkness. When St. Clair tucked the pistol back into his waistband, Buckley said, "You're efficient with that. Ranier was one of the strongest of the Southern troublemakers." He sighed and nipped the end from a cigar, then passed the box to St. Clair and Delaney. "Officially, I can only commend you but personally, I am censuring your impetuous actions for had you failed to carry them off the whole mission could have collapsed. I am warning you for the second time — curb yourself in the future. We go by the book here!"

St. Clair leaned forward on Buckley's desk. "Very well sir, but as I saw it the situation called for drastic action. That load of buckshot was aimed at my head and it was hardly the time to seek official approval." He lit his cigar over the lamp chimney. Settling back again, he said, "I've been here less than two weeks, yet Royce had the word on me. Where's the leak, sir? There is one — a bad one."

"I don't know," Buckley admitted. He gnawed on his cigar.

"Did you know I was coming?" St. Clair asked.

Buckley paused with his smoke half-raised. "Yes. I knew a Point man was coming, but not your name. What are you driving at?"

St. Clair shook his head and spoke to Delaney. "Sergeant, did you know my name when you boarded the train?"

"No, lad," Delaney said. "I was told I'd recognize you by the raincape and Major Delafield's pistol."

"Neither of you knew me, and surely Jim Overmile didn't," St. Clair mused. "Yet Royce has a crystal ball and singles me out right away. At least well enough for Ranier to try to kill me."

"I think I see what you're getting at," Buckley said softly. "You think the leak's farther up the line?"

"It's possible," St. Clair said. He stood up. "If you'll excuse me, sir, I think I'll get some rest."

"Get all you can," Buckley said. "We're moving out tomorrow evening. That information is between us."

St. Clair saluted and let himself out onto the darkened parade. There were no lights at all in the barracks as he found his bunk quietly and undressed.

After reveille the troopers began to police the area and squads were detailed. The escort wagons were checked, the quartermaster mule trains made ready, and at the remount stables, St. Clair and Jim Overmile were assigned to the squad that selected horses.

After the evening mess the bugler blew officers' call and an hour later the troopers were formed in ranks and the moving out began. C Troop left the stockade first, Lieutenant Buckley heading the column. Behind, came E Troop with Royce in command, then Lieutenant Chambers with D, and Lieutenant McAuliff forming the rear guard with B.

The quartermaster mule train, along with the escort wagons bearing the heavier equipment, followed a mile behind. Chains jangled in the night and the ammonia of horses mingled with the sharp odor of dust. Buckley used the general cavalry march orders: halt fifteen minutes during the hour, dismount and unbit for grazing. Trot five minutes after every half hour of walking to avoid animal fatigue and lessen the possibility of back sores due to bad carriage in the saddle. Dismount and lead ten minutes out of every hour.

Dust foamed waist-high and powdered the men to the hips, showering a white mantle on shoulders and masking their faces. Leather protested as rumps hit cold saddles. There were no sounds save the necessary clank of equipment and the dull pop of hooves in the dust.

Moving north, they cut through the land and over low, rolling hills, all heavily wooded. Ride, walk, housekeeping stops. They bivouacked late.

Lieutenant Buckley gave his orders quietly: "Dismount and unsaddle. This is bivouac, Sergeant Delaney. Night grazing area is between the military crest of that slope and the dry wash. Picket pins — no rope on the ground tonight."

The bright cells of squad fires sprang up and men gathered around them, preparing their own meals. Guard detail was selected and posted. The camp bedded down for the night. Buckley kept the troops separated and had officers' call soon after the meal. Royce, because of his position of command, attended this meeting. Buckley gave no sign of any suspicions he harbored against the sullen sergeant.

As soon as the sky began to lighten the troops were called to saddle and mount. With so many raw recruits, the handful of officers and noncoms worked and cursed until the ranks were formed.

Buckley's command floated back from the head of the column: "Prepare to mount! *Mount!*" Leather creaked and horses shied nervously. "Forward by twooos! *Hoooo!*"

Behind C Troop, E, D, and B gagged in the dust. Throughout the morning they clung to the monotonous march orders and by midafternoon they scudded down off the slanting hillside that dipped to the wide Missouri River, sparkling in the sun.

Near a sheltered, natural landing, six steam packets were moored in a line. They were relatively small, no more than fifty-five feet long, for in this treacherous river with its shifting bottom no large boat could venture without risk.

Smoke spouted from the high black stacks and on the decks men shifted back and forth, making ready to receive cargo. Wide gangplanks were dropped in place and Buckley ordered the four troops to dismount.

One detail fought the horses aboard, which consumed the better part of an hour. The quartermaster mule train arrived and was loaded aboard one packet. Escort wagons were wheeled up, unhitched and muscled aboard. With wagons and animals picketed in the well decks of the first two packets, one troop marched aboard each boat to handle the stock.

Toward evening, the lead packet carrying half the mules and horses, gave a brief blast on the whistle and the bow lines were cast off. Edging out into midstream, the paddlewheels began to churn the muddy water to a froth. On the Texas deck, Lieutenant McAuliff consulted the captain and they hove to, standing out from shore, the paddlewheel turning slowly to maintain their position against the current.

The second packet, also loaded with animals, cast off its lines. Lieutenant Chambers was in command and he pulled alongside the first vessel and waited while the other boats edged into the stream. Two of the packets were loaded with quartermaster supplies and Buckley signaled them to go ahead. Ten minutes later they steamed out of sight past a bend upstream. These two, ferrying quartermaster troops, would steam straight through to Kansas City.

When Buckley's packet edged past, the other two strung out behind him and they began to make way up river. The vessels stayed close, no more than cable's length apart. Sergeant Royce and E Troop occupied the second packet.

They continued on their course until an hour after full dark, when the captain gave two sharp jerks on the whistle cord and edged the prow of the boat toward the dark outline of a low island. The packet shuddered as the prow moored on the muddy beach.

Buckley summoned his trumpeter. Officers' call was blown and when they gathered on the lead packet's Texas, Buckley said, "No one leaves the packets. I know it will be uncomfortable but we'll have to make the best of it. Cold rations. Half rations for the horses, a full one for the mules. That's all, gentlemen."

In the morning the men fell out with the sun and before a full dawn broke, the packets were again nosing against the current. Through the rest of the day the men lazed around and talked. One monotonous hour dragged into the next and the troopers began to chafe at the inactivity. Their close proximity to one another intensified small dislikes until they threatened to become full-blown antipathies. Although the second day dawned peacefully enough, by noon three fights had broken out, two on Lieutenant Chambers' boat and one on Lieutenant McAuliff's packet. All were squelched before any damage could be done, but later the officers had reason to ponder the wisdom of this prompt action. The troopers were in sore need of releasing pent up energy, and denied this natural outlet, they grew more discontented.

Buckley lacked experienced officers. He'd served nine years on the frontier and realized that only time could instill the power of command in some men. Always he watched Sergeant Royce and did not fail to notice that the sergeant maintained almost perfect control over his men, while both McAuliff and Chambers had difficulty. McAuliff made an attempt to organize exercises among the troopers on his packet but the response was so sullen that he lost heart and surrendered the idea. This defeat cost him his last vestige of control and Buckley cursed under his breath. A more experienced officer would have demanded obedience and in the process would have restored the full power of his command.

Buckley watched over his brood with a troubled eye, waiting for the unavoidable explosion. Sergeant Delaney was constantly at his side. They stood on the aft rail of the Texas deck, observing the discontent seething on the other boats.

CHAPTER 5

On the third day the weather turned muggy and the animosity increased among the troopers. A layer of thick clouds all but blotted out the sun and the humidity built up.

Quincy St. Clair was standing apart from the others by the lee side of the afterdeck when Sergeant Delaney came down the ladder from the Texas. St. Clair said, "Don't light a match, Sergeant. This is about ready to go off by itself."

"That's likely," Delaney said soberly. "I've been wondering what's been holding it together this long." He nodded toward the Texas deck. "Peg's aboard. She has the mate's cabin aft the wheelhouse. Go on up. Buckley wants to see you."

"Is he there now?"

Delaney shook his head. "He'll be along directly."

St. Clair went up the narrow companionway and disappeared forward. The Texas was narrow and not too long; he moved toward the wheelhouse and the cabins behind it. Tapping on the door, he listened to her footsteps, and then the door opened.

Peg smiled and said, "Forbidden territory to a trooper, Quincy. Don't you know that?"

"Official business," he said, and swept off his forager cap to make a slight bow.

She glanced past him and listened to the silence on the deck below, her forehead puckering in a frown. She said, "What's happening down there?"

"They'll be at each other's throats by nightfall," he told her.

"The way I feel that's a long way off," she said, and invited him in. The cabin was small and he squatted against the bulkhead while she sat on the bottom bunk, leaning forward to let her head clear the rails of the top. "This morning the captain said there were Sioux along the river. That might break the monotony."

"The choice is equally bad," he said. "A Sioux warrior or a discontented soldier." He smiled. "What do you think of the new assignment?"

She shrugged. "I don't think of assignments, Quincy. The Army's the Army, at Mincanopy with the Second Dragoons against the Seminoles in 'thirty-six, Bent's Fort to Santa Fe in 'forty-six, or Contreras and all the way to Aqua Fria with Winfield Scott."

"But it's not what you want," St. Clair said wisely. "You don't like to travel on a pigboat while officers' wives go in style."

She studied him seriously for a moment. "You're more observing than I gave you credit for. But you're very foolish. Sergeant Royce is still free. Are you asking for it again?"

"Royce isn't the top man," he said. "We agreed to give him rope." He raised a hand and wiped the perspiration from his face. The air was thick with heat and breathing was a chore. His wool uniform clung to him and he had the rank gaminess of a trooper now.

Peg said, "You don't like this, do you? Pretending to be a trooper."

"Have I complained?"

"No, but I sense the resentment. It must be galling to take orders from men you feel superior to. Is that why you defied Buckley's order and tangled with Royce and Rance Ranier?"

"I had one reprimand for that. Do I deserve another?" He shook his head in exasperation. "Peg, why do we have to misunderstand each other?"

"Do we? I thought I understood *you*."

He stood up and bumped his head on the wooden knee that braced the pilot-house floor. "I'd better go back to the well deck where I belong," he said.

"You don't belong there either," Peg said honestly. "You belong on the quarterdeck in command. But that would be a waste. You'd get yourself killed in your first campaign."

"Pity?" He didn't know whether to be amused or troubled by her concern.

She shook her head. "I don't pity anyone, Quincy. A man makes himself with what tools are handy. He uses ambition, luck, whatever he can find, but he's the craftsman with the final say."

"You're a strange girl, Peg. Deep. I like that, but often I get the impression that you're trying to fit me in some special category you have in your mind."

"Maybe I am," she said. "You don't have much faith in anything and I seem to resent it personally when I know I shouldn't."

"I don't follow you."

"Your girl. You assumed from the beginning that she wouldn't believe in you. Was it because you find it so hard to believe in yourself? Sometimes pretending that others are that way too makes a person less lonely."

103

"It seems," he said, "that you are judging something you know nothing about."

"Am I?" She smiled. "I lost my mother when I was four. I've been around men all my life and I see a lot. But I'm picking on a small point, am I not? I'm a woman, and because of your snap judgment of another, I feel a reflected slight. I can't help thinking that you would think of me with equal levity if I were in her place."

"But you're not in her place," he told her, and turned again to the cabin door.

She took his arm quickly. "Are you going away angry?"

"No. Just wiser."

"Now you're talking over *my* head," Peg admitted.

"I'm beginning to figure you out," St. Clair said. "You're lying to yourself, Peg. Pretending to be happy living on Suds Row — having some fresh lieutenant's wife ask you to do her laundry. That's all a lie, Peg. You want to sit in your own parlor in a white dress and have silver on the table. You want it real bad. There's a lot you want but you know a sergeant's pay will never get it for you and you can't marry an officer while your father's in the Army. You keep harping on the idea that I look down my nose at a trooper. Isn't that the way you imagine everyone looks at you because you're a trooper's daughter? You shouldn't push your feelings off on me because it pinches you to have them. Are you afraid of sounding disloyal to your father because of the way you feel?"

She stared at him, her eyes wide and startled. Then the door opened and Lieutenant Buckley stepped in, sweeping off his hat. He glanced at St. Clair and his voice was momentarily sharp, "A social call?"

Sergeant Delaney's heavy boots pounded up the companionway and he squeezed inside and closed the door. He said, "A little tight in here for a board meetin', sor."

Buckley looked at Peg Delaney. "Can you keep your mouth shut?"

"Jules," she said, "if I told all I know about the Army, sixty percent of the officers would be drummed out tomorrow morning."

"I see," Buckley said, and smiled, his finger brushing his mustache. He turned on St. Clair. "Try and find a place to squat. When you stand at attention it reminds me of a Prussian colonel we had when I was at the Point. Have you anything to drink in here, Sergeant?"

Buckley shied his hat onto the top bunk,

then sat down on the small stool by the pull-out desk.

"There's a bottle in the drawer, sor. Medicinal purposes, of course."

"I feel as if I've taken a touch of the pip," Buckley said dryly. He took the bottle, drinking deeply before popping the cork back in the neck. Tempered and full of self confidence though he was, Buckley fully understood his own weaknesses and limitations. Glancing at St. Clair, he asked, "What would you do in Lieutenant McAuliff's place? He no longer has any control over his troop."

"I think I'd promote a fight, sir," St. Clair said. "Sort of clear the air. Then I'd step in and whip the winner. Any man who opened his mouth would get it smashed, respectfully, sir."

Buckley smiled. "That answer fits you to a tee. But under the circumstances it just might do the trick. I have half a notion to relieve McAuliff and let you straighten out those men." He paused to wipe perspiration from his face. "Don't mind what I say. McAuliff's a good man but he's a dandy. Hates to get his hands dirty." He raised his eyes again to St. Clair. "Tell me about the Point. Is Captain Holmes still teaching math?"

"He's still there, sir. The Point hasn't changed."

"I guess not," Buckley said softly. "I hated it the first year I was there, but after awhile it got me. There's something about the sunlight on the Plain and the cadets on parade." He paused to search his pockets for a cigar, found one, and discovered it was crushed. "I can still see the buildings with ivy climbers on the walls. Even when I rode the riding ring with blood running down my legs, I wouldn't have had it different. Is that the way you felt about it, St. Clair?"

"Yes, sir. All the time."

"I remember the chapel bells," Buckley said. "Made a man get religion, those bells." He slapped his thighs and stood up. "The Point is a beautiful place, but I wish to hell they'd take the officers' corps out of the ranks." He gave Sergeant Delaney a rap on the arm. "Thanks for the drink. I never knew an Irishman who didn't have good whiskey."

He opened the door, stepped half out, then paused. "St. Clair, keep a sharp eye on Royce and his men." He hesitated, then added, "And do me a favor. This time go by the book. Less confusing that way."

"You think something's —"

"I'm just being prepared," Buckley said, and went out.

Sergeant Delaney lingered a moment longer, then left. Peg said nothing and St. Clair turned toward the door. She touched his arm and brought his head around. She said, "Quincy, I'm sorry. Sometimes the truth hurts."

"I never wanted to hurt you, Peg."

A whistle tooted and he went to the cabin window to look out. Buckley's packet was slowing, allowing McAuliff and Chambers to pull ahead. The river was wide here and obviously shallow, for the brown shoulders of sandbars thrust past the surface.

He turned back and faced her. "Peg, I don't think we'd bother to scratch at each other all the time if —"

"Don't say it!" She lowered her eyes and sat down quickly. "I know what you want to say and I don't want to hear it. Not now or at any other time. You're too much like someone I once knew."

"Is falling in love that painful a prospect?" He asked this softly and saw her stiffen. He opened the door then. "All right, Peg. All right." He closed the door and stepped to the Texas deck.

The shrill blast of the packet's whistle

made him jump and men on the deck below began to yell. Coming from a distance, the spasmodic crackle of musketry sounded like a raging brush fire.

Racing to the edge of the Texas, St. Clair saw the line of mounted Indians along the bank. The distance was sixty yards and all along the shore, puffs of gray smoke erupted and musket balls pimpled the water, struck the wood hull, and thudded against flesh in the well deck.

"Po-sitions!" Buckley shouted. "Fire by squad!"

Glass shattered in the pilothouse as a ball screamed through and the captain's angry shooting was an immediate answer. He stood in full view of the line of warriors, his corncob pipe clenched in his teeth, and fired his Dragoon pistol with absurd daring.

In the well deck, troopers dropped into place along the low gunwales. An answering fire began. The yelling of the Indians was clear now, rolling over the crack of carbine fire. Up ahead, Lieutenant McAuliff's packet began to slow, then the paddlewheel stopped abruptly. McAuliff was running back and forth on the Texas, rallying his men, but confusion held them and the Indians seemed to sense this. They

109

splashed into the water away from the shore, closed the range to twenty-five yards and laid a withering fire of bullets and arrows over the helpless packet.

Some brave succeeded in launching a fire arrow into the wheelhouse. The captain and mate beat a hasty retreat while McAuliff made a desperate attempt to organize a fire brigade.

On the packet behind, Chambers cursed McAuliff in a shrill voice, knowing that the lead vessel would soon drift into the strong current and be carried back into the path of the other boats.

Chambers tried to turn his packet but the Sioux concentrated such an attack on the wheelhouse that the captain and crew had to withdraw. Weathering the severe fire, Lieutenant Chambers rose to the tradition of the corps and entered the wheelhouse. He was shot through the body almost instantly.

He fell but got up and twisted the huge wheel, trying to swing the packet cross channel in an attempt to abort the drifting lead packet's course. His was a gallant effort for the Sioux screamed exultantly and threw themselves against the vessel with renewed effort.

From the well deck of Buckley's packet,

C Troop tried to answer them but the positions of the boats were such that they could bring no more than a quarter of their firepower to bear on the Indians.

Buckley ordered the power cut, for the boats were close together now. The lead packet struck Chambers' ship with a crash that sent torn timbers flying. The lieutenant, still in the wheelhouse and bleeding profusely, locked his arms over the spokes and died.

On Sergeant Royce's boat, several troopers invaded the wheelhouse, shot the captain and mate and turned the packet away from the fight. E Troop grimly lined the port rail, carbines leveled at Buckley's packet. Their fire was a scythe that dropped five men in the first volley.

"Mutiny!" Delaney shouted. He stood helpless as another withering fire swept Buckley's packet. Some soldiers, repelled by Royce's conspiracy, jumped overboard and tried for the safety of Buckley's ship. The two lead packets, hopelessly smashed together, began drifting toward Buckley, who called frantically for the captain to reverse the engine.

Royce had turned almost completely about, and the Sioux joined him in sending a wave of firepower against Buckley that left his boat without control. The troopers in the well deck were fighting hopeless odds and the crew fled from the wheelhouse as the Sioux concentrated their attack there.

With his packet swinging to the current, Buckley could only brace himself against the crush as the two lead boats stove in the bow with a rending of timbers. The jar knocked troopers asprawl and the three boats were now thoroughly enmeshed, beyond hope of control.

Royce had pulled clear, and with him, the Sioux. They stood off and laid a devastating fire over the crippled packets. Troopers made a gallant attempt to answer, but without organization their fire was ragged and ill-directed.

Lieutenant Buckley, still standing on the Texas, saw that Royce and the Sioux were in league and swore that he would even this score at another time. His ship was sinking beneath his feet. Already she was heavy in the bow and settling fast. The paddlewheel suddenly struck a submerged log which ruptured half the blades, while the first packet sank to the bottom and the troopers took to the water.

The animals were in complete panic, creating almost as much havoc as the

Sioux and mutineer rifles. Some floundered in the water while others thrashed about the deck, stepping on troopers, falling and breaking bones.

The first packet had now settled sufficiently for water to reach her boilers and the explosion shook all three boats as she split asunder and died with her Texas and wheelhouse awash.

Royce's packet was standing out a hundred yards away, and his men were still firing. The shriek of Indians, the screaming of men and animals and the hoarse rattle of rifle and musket all combined to lay such a cacophony over the river that a shouted command could not be heard.

"Trumpeter!" Buckley bellowed. "Sound recall and put some spit into it!" He felt the deck shift beneath his feet and wondered how many seconds he had before the river reached the boilers.

The troopers on the second packet heard the sharp ring of the C horn and went over the side a moment before the packet exploded. Over the crashing of weapons and the wild shouting of men the spry tones of the bugle broke through and men abandoned ship.

Sergeant Royce was pulling away downstream, the Sioux trailing him along the shore. Buckley left the Texas three steps at a time as St. Clair abandoned his position by the larboard rail.

Sergeant Delaney was nowhere in sight. Buckley called orders to the troopers. He saw St. Clair and altered his course to yell, "For God's sake, get Peg! This tub's going up any minute. Make shore and rejoin us there. I'll wait for you!"

The second packet was now afire and listing badly to one side. Several of the escort wagons broke free to rumble across the deck and crash into the side of the pilothouse. St. Clair went up the companionway at a run. From this height he could see the whole scene, and he flattened himself against the wheelhouse wall as a new explosion shook the world. He crouched against the bullet-pocked wheelhouse as boards and splinters rained around him, his mind divining the source of the blast. One of the escort wagons loaded with paper patch ammunition had crashed into the flaming wheelhouse of the boat ahead.

He looked around at the men in the water. Some were struck by flying debris and sank from sight. Others fought the current and the wildly thrashing horses. The packet was listing badly as St. Clair put his shoulder against the door to Peg's

114

cabin. He pushed it inward a foot, then felt it stick. Dropping to his knees, he thrust an arm inside and found Peg Delaney on the floor. St. Clair shoved hard on the door to push her back and made his way inside.

Dropping to her side, he shook her and heard her moan. There was no time to be gentle so he slapped her smartly until she regained consciousness. She raised her hand to the bump on her head. "The jar," she mumbled. "I fell. Hit my head."

"We've got to get out of here." He lifted her to her feet. "We'll have to go over the side."

She grabbed at the door frame and clung tightly. "But I can't swim!"

"I'll teach you," he said, and struck her hands away. Hustling her to the lee rail, he stopped. The water below was swarming with men and animals and a jump of twenty feet might injure them both. Taking her arm, he pulled her around the wrecked pilothouse to the other side. The boat settled sharply and their feet slid along the deck.

"Get rid of your shoes," he ordered, pulling off his own heavy boots. He glanced down at the ankle-length, highbuttoned shoes she wore and knew there would not be time. Almost savagely

115

he pushed her into the water and dived after her.

She had not lied to him; she could not swim. He caught her as she sank and when they broke the surface she began to claw at him. Without hesitation he belted her stiffly along the jawline with his fist. She went limp, and he began to paddle toward the far shore. He made his calculations against the strong pull of the current, growing alarmed when he found that they were drifting excessively. Finally he realized that Peg's heavy skirt was an impossible drag, and fumbling beneath the water, he ripped it away.

Buckley's packet exploded with a muffled boom, sending up a spout of water and mud. The wreckage settled on the bottom with the Texas nearly awash. Timbers flew at them from the sky and St. Clair dived, taking Peg Delaney with him. When he surfaced again, she was choking and spitting water.

Nearby, a deck beam floated with the current and he paddled to it. Peg clung to it while he tied her with his belt. Then he pushed them toward shore as darkness began to filter over the land.

The Sioux were far downstream now and Sergeant Royce's stolen packet was hove to in midstream. On the far shore the first of the survivors were dragging themselves up the muddy banks. St. Clair wondered if Lieutenant Buckley had made it. It would be a nearly impossible task to reorganize the scattered forces. Then his mind became absorbed in his battle with the current. When finally his feet touched bottom, he inched his way onto a sandbar that jutted out from a wooded cove. A few minutes later he untied Peg from the timber and helped her onto dry land. She wanted to stop and rest but he forced her into motion, saying, "Not here!" New as he was to this hostile land, and unschooled in its ways, he realized that they must have cover.

She took several halting steps and stumbled. He put his hands beneath her arms and hoisted her to her feet. Her wet blouse and shift barely reached to mid-thigh and clung in sodden folds.

"I can't go on," Peg said. "I'm sick."

Quincy put his arm around her and hurried her through the brush. The branches tore at her, whipping welts against her bare arms and legs. He tried to move cautiously, to make as little noise as possible, but haste pressed against him and he became clumsy.

117

Coming to a creek that flowed to the Missouri, St. Clair followed its ragged path until he reached a hilly section that was screened by heavy brush and timber. Peg Delaney's teeth began to chatter as soon as they stopped. St. Clair took off his wool shirt and made her slip it on. She clutched the damp cloth about her but seemed to shiver just as badly.

Common sense warned him that he shouldn't light a fire in this predicament, but Peg's condition demanded warmth. He gathered twigs and dried branches. He kept the blaze as small as possible and she huddled over it until her shivering abated. The warmth seemed to thaw some of the daze from her mind and she rubbed her bare legs where branches had switched her. "What happened to my skirt and petticoats?" she asked as though suddenly aware of their loss. Then she moved her jaw experimentally. "You hit me too, didn't you?"

"Hit you and tore off your dress," he said. "It was dragging us under." He tried to smile and found that he could. "Have I compromised you, Peg?"

Some of her humor returned and she pulled the tail of his shirt over her tucked-up knees. "My father will buy a shotgun."

Her hair had come unbound and hung in wet ropes over her shoulders. With a woman's patience she began to press the water from it.

St. Clair took inventory of their situation and found himself too short for comfort. His cap and ball Colt might be useless. If water had leaked in around the nipples and fouled the powder, it wouldn't fire. He had three waxed matches left, and no boots. The wooden box holding twelve paper cartridges for his Colt would dry out providing he could spread them on a piece of bark and let them lie in the sun come daylight, but that would take too long and he couldn't wait.

The stinging welts on Peg's legs pushed her modesty aside and she rubbed them again. In the firelight they were bold red streaks against the whiteness of her flesh. A deep darkness filled the woods around them. Finally she said, "Did my father get away all right?"

"I don't know," St. Clair said soberly. "The last I saw of him he was rallying the troopers. Then Buckley ordered everybody over the side."

"What happened Quincy? I hit my head when the packets collided."

"Royce pulled another trick," he said,

"and this time he carried it off. Somebody must have enlisted the aid of the Sioux because they created the diversion while Royce and his mutineers ran off with the packet. If they hadn't opened fire —" He waved his hand impatiently. "What's the difference now? It happened. All I know is, we have to get out of here and damn soon."

"You've no boots," Peg said. "You can't walk far without them."

"We'll stay here awhile," he said, and kicked out the fire. He lay on the ground beside her. "We'll try to work our way upstream and cross the river somehow. Lieutenant Buckley will be gathering the survivors and we'll get re-outfitted and march to Kansas City."

"In my — this way?" She was very indignant. "I won't stand to have all those soldiers gawk at me!"

"I'll leave you on the bank," he said, "and bring you back some trousers." He rolled over and looked around at the dark land. He could see nothing, but he knew the Sioux were out there and it made him jumpy.

"You want your shirt back?" She spoke in a small voice.

"Keep it. You'll be cold." He lay back

and pulled her down beside him for warmth. She lay stiffly for a few minutes, then relaxed.

Huddled together, they shared a meager warmth and for a while she dozed. St. Clair found sleep impossible. He thought, *she didn't stay scared long, but I'm still scared. Talk about green officers . . . I don't even know where I am.*

Time passed with agonizing languor. What he judged to be two hours later — the water had stopped his watch — he bent over Peg, bringing her awake with a touch of his hand. Suspecting that she might cry out, he covered her mouth with his hand. When he felt her relax he took his hand away. The night was not so dark now for pale moonlight filtered through the trees. He could see her face vaguely, a pale oval. He said, "In case I never get another chance —" and kissed her gently on the lips.

The soft pillow of her mouth remained passive for a moment, and then some strong resolve melted away and she flung her arms around him and lifted herself to him. Time stopped while they clung together, and then her arms fell away and he sat back, shaken.

"He almost needed that shotgun," he

said, pulling her to her feet. She leaned against him briefly, her body warm and soft, and afterward he wondered if it had been a caress or if weariness had made her lean for support.

He took her hand and guided her through the creek bed. An hour later they reached the bank of the river. St. Clair felt that he was below the wrecked packets and turned upstream, moving with exaggerated caution. Mud made traveling difficult and Peg stopped to rid herself of her ruined shoes. When they stopped again for a short rest, St. Clair calculated that they must be about a mile above the wrecked packets by now and if he swam across from here the current would carry him near them or slightly above.

There was no wreckage here for Peg to cling to so he led her into the water until it reached her breast and said, "Put your arms around my neck but don't choke me. Stay as still as you can and you'll float. I'll get you across."

"And if we don't —"

"We will."

She laid her head against his chest. "Thank you, Quincy."

He understood that she was referring to the kiss. He suddenly wanted to kiss her again, but instead he put his arm around her and pushed away toward the opposite shore.

He swam on his side in a half dog-paddle, and by the time he went halfway he knew the job was too much for him. Peg's weight dragged him and the current deflected his course. He had to battle constantly to maintain a heading. His arms and legs began to ache with the strain and his rhythm faltered.

She felt him weaken and said, "I'll let go before I cause you to drown."

A fear that she might do this pierced his mind and he rolled over on his other side, his left arm encircling her waist. Swimming blindly, he did not see the sunken hull of the last packet resting on the mud bottom. His head slammed against the side of the Texas deck with enough force to stun him but he rallied and groped along the side for a hand-hold.

Peg held on while he climbed onto the Texas, now not more than a foot out of the water. He went belly-flat on the listing deck and stretched his arms down for her. She climbed wearily out and they stood dripping and looking around them.

In the dim light they could see that the

larboard side of the Texas deck was awash. The two packets ahead were dark shapes jumbled together, the first almost completely submerged. He pushed Peg ahead of him and entered the captain's quarters aft of the bullet-riddled wheelhouse. He fumbled around in the darkness until he found the bunks.

Taking a heavy blanket from the upper one, he said, "Take off those wet clothes and wrap this around you."

Her nerves were like an E string and she seized on this, deliberately distorting his meaning so she could use it as a vent for her emotions. "I certainly will not!"

"Peg," he said patiently, "I haven't the time to argue with you." His hand came out and fastened in the cloth at her throat and with one yank he tore it from her. She struck at him, forgetting herself completely. Blocking her flailing hands, he slapped her and she quieted with shocking suddenness. Then, supporting her with one arm, he draped the blanket around her. She did not seem able to stand so he slipped one arm behind her knees and lifted her into the lower bunk.

She began crying then.

He stood there a moment, uncertain of his next move. Finally her crying stopped and she said, "I'm all right, Quincy. I'm sorry."

"I'll be back," he told her. "I'm going to swim ashore and see what's happened to the command."

He slipped out and a short time later she heard the splash as he went over the side. Her face ached where he had struck her and a lump was beginning to form on the hinge of her jaw. For a time she battled the loneliness that threatened to engulf her, and then she gave in to it. She wanted to cry his name and bring him back. He would come back if she called. She knew he would.

But she couldn't do that. He knew her now for a weak woman who lost all control in an emergency. Her pride was shattered. He would help her but later he would remember her weakness.

No he wouldn't. He wasn't like that.

She had learned a great deal about Quincy St. Clair in these last hectic hours. He was strong, not only physically, but emotionally, and he could face a crisis with calm efficiency.

He'll make a good officer, she thought. He'd make a good husband. . . . Now why did I think of that? She clung to the remembrance of his kiss, but still she felt that he didn't love her. He was merely gallant; he knew women well enough to kiss them when they most needed it.

Peg turned over in the bunk and the wool blanket felt rough against her body. *I shouldn't have flared up at him,* she thought. Even as she had lashed out at him with words she'd known that he was thinking only of her welfare. A sharp sense of shame filled her. Then a new thought struck her. *If only he'd touched me with . . . awareness. . . .*

But he hadn't. He'd kissed her only because he wanted her to know that half-drowned, in danger, he'd still felt their significance as man and woman.

Why didn't he touch me?

She lay for a long time wondering, then sat up as she heard his feet pad softly on the deck. He entered the cabin, his hand reaching for her. "Peg?" he said.

She stirred beneath his hand and he squatted on the slanting floor. "We'll have to make it alone, Peg. Buckley and the troops have pulled out."

126

CHAPTER 6

Lieutenant Jules Buckley viewed his military career with a great deal of seriousness and the defeat he had suffered at the hands of Sergeant Royce and the Sioux brought tears to his eyes. This emotion did not spring from any well of self pity, but rather from the outraged anger a man feels when, after taking reasonable precautions, he still finds himself outwitted.

Composing himself, Buckley called to his trumpeter, who was standing near by, shaking water from his C horn. "Assembly," he said gruffly, "and sound it with a flourish." He turned as Sergeant Delaney came up.

All along the river bank men and animals were pulling themselves onto dry land. Many more men were still in the water, some floating lifelessly, while others floundered because of wounds. The men who gained the shore immediately began to gather animals. A natural sense of order seemed to take over.

"Have you made a casualty check yet?"

Buckley asked, touching his kepi visor in answer to Delaney's salute.

"A quick one, sor," Delaney said. "We're in bad shape. A twenty percent loss, sor. A good fifty percent off the horse books."

Lieutenant Buckley's shock was obvious. "That bad?"

The bugler sounded assembly and men rallied to the blaring tones. Lieutenant McAuliff hurried up, his soggy uniform clinging to him. He saluted and Buckley said, "Details to gather what horses and mules you can. We'll vacate this position in two hours."

"But, sir — what of Sergeant Royce and the mutineers?"

Buckley's face was severe. "Mr. McAuliff, I am perfectly aware of Sergeant Royce's acts. Rest assured that he will be shot for this. Now we haven't time for a debating society. Get on with it."

"Yes, sir," McAuliff said. "Sir, I hold myself solely responsible for this misadventure."

"Nonsense," Buckley snapped. "Get back with the men and get some organization into this thing."

After McAuliff moved away, Delaney's worry found voice. "My daughter, sor. I — couldn't leave my post, sor."

"St. Clair went to her," Buckley said. "I saw him, Sergeant. I'm sure he got her off in time." He put his hand on Delaney's shoulder. "He's a capable man. She'll be all right with him."

"Yes, sor," Delaney said. "Maybe they made the other side, sor. I don't see 'em here." He peered through the deepening gloom of the coming night, but with so much confusion on the river bank it was difficult to identify anyone. "I'll get on with the men, sor," he said, and moved away.

Lieutenant Buckley watched him for a moment, wishing he could reassure him, but he had no way of knowing whether St. Clair and the girl had reached safety. The current could have swept them downstream. Perhaps they had drowned. He pushed the thought from his mind. St. Clair was young and inexperienced but he had a flair for turning the odds in a bad situation. The outcome of the fight with Rance Ranier had convinced Buckley of this.

He forced his mind back to the problem of salvaging what he could from the melee and plunged into the task with a fury that prohibited speculation on Peg Delaney's fate. Nine of the quartermaster mules were located and picketed. Twenty-one sound horses were caught. An ordnance check revealed that more than half the men had lost their carbines in the grim battle to reach shore.

Buckley considered the possibility of Sergeant Royce returning and thought it unlikely, for the Sioux would not attack at night and Royce's force was not strong enough to win a hand-to-hand fight.

Royce would gain nothing from another attack. He had stopped the troops from reaching the frontier and that had been his goal. When the Sioux had withdrawn so suddenly, Buckley had been momentarily puzzled. Then he realized that Royce must have bought the Indians' loyalty for trade muskets and powder. He could hardly blame the Indians.

In an hour the camp was fairly well organized. All equipment not needed was abandoned. Buckley called to Lieutenant McAuliff. "Get me ten men who can swim. There are still muskets and ammunition on the river bottom. The weapons can be dried and the paper-patch ammunition is in waterproof boxes. I want enough for each man to be armed with a full ration of powder."

"Yes, sir," McAuliff said. He hurried away, calling for volunteers.

A group of men stripped down and entered the water with a dozen more following. For twenty minutes the troopers dived and surfaced, bringing up carbines and cartons of ammunition which they passed to the men on shore.

Darkness smothered the land as Buckley ordered litters fashioned for the wounded. The able-bodied would walk and the wounded would be transported on travois behind the horses while the less severely injured rode.

There were eighty-five men, seventy of these in fighting condition. Calling once again to McAuliff, Buckley said, "We'll march on to Kansas City to join our reenforcements. Pass the order back to move out quietly, Mister."

The order crept down the column and slowly the troopers began to come alive. The thought of their predicament hung like a pall over Buckley's mind, try as he would to shake it off. Afoot in hostile country . . . cold rations . . . the minimum of ammunition . . . wounded to care for.

Would they ever make it?

St. Clair found the tenacious captain dead in the wheelhouse, his corncob pipe lying by his head. One hand still clutched a

Dragoon revolver and St. Clair felt somewhat cheered as he lifted the massive gun. The eight-inch barrel had been shortened to six inches and St. Clair discovered the reason when he found the captain's shoulder holster in the chart cabinet. Now armed with dry ammunition, St. Clair felt a renewed optimism for the future. He returned to the captain's cabin and found Peg Delaney shivering in her sleep. Covering her with another blanket, he searched through the captain's wardrobe for dry clothes for himself. Then carrying these to the Texas, he stowed them for future use and dived over the side, swimming for the shore twenty yards away.

He raised himself, dripping, to the muddy bank and moved around in the dark until he found Buckley's old camp, marked by scattered debris and a significant row of unmarked graves.

Combing through the discarded supplies, he found trousers and shirt for Peg and laid them on the bank. From the brush along the river he pulled large timbers, and when he had enough, he stripped the harness leather from the dead mules to lash his raft together.

Returning once more to the deserted camp, he looked for anything he might be able to use, finally finding a carbine with a cracked stock, and a bullet pouch holding four packets of paper cartridges, the wax seals unbroken. These would fire, he told himself, and went on until he uncovered a case of soggy rations.

He stacked this booty on the shore, put the dry clothing on the raft and paddled through the darkness toward the sunken packet. Searching the stars, he judged the time to be near midnight or later when he again boarded the Texas. He exchanged his own wet clothing for that of the captain, relishing their dry warmth, then took the things he had brought for Peg and returned to the captain's cabin. Opening the door he went in and bumped into Peg Delaney standing unsteadily in the middle of the small room. His arms enfolded her instinctively and he felt her hot flesh.

She was burning with fever!

The touch of his hands aroused her and she tried to strike him but he fended off the aimless blows and forced her to the cabin floor. She squirmed and struggled as he dressed her, frantic in her delirium.

"Don't, Jim!" Her hands shoved at him as he buttoned the shirt. "You said you loved me, and I believed you. . . ." He fought her kicking feet into the trousers and leaned on her chest to quiet her as he pulled them on. "Jim, I hate you . . . you're hurting me. . . ."

Kneeling by her side, he cinched the belt around her waist. Suddenly she lashed out at him with a new fury that propelled him back to the wall. Getting to her feet, she raced for the door and he blocked her just in time. She was panting and crying when he locked an arm about her, lifting her clear of the floor.

"No, Jim! You never wanted to marry me, did you? Not like this, please . . . not like this. . . ."

She sank against him with a moan and he managed to hook the suspenders over her shoulders, trying to shorten them to an efficient length. He felt a wave of despair as he realized how ill she was, and had to abandon all hope of following Buckley tonight.

Carrying Peg to the bunk St. Clair tied her in with a small coil of rope. Her ravings were getting louder and he searched the wardrobe again for a handkerchief to tie over her mouth. When he went out again, he could hear her subdued moaning as she fought the bonds.

He made another trip to shore by raft, and returned to the dry side of the Texas deck with his gathered supplies. He hung blankets over the broken cabin windows, then used his bayonet to cut the side from a canteen. With some water-soaked planks, St. Clair improvised a bed for the canteen and made a small fire in it. Cutting the side from another canteen, he formed a shallow bowl and in this cooked a beef jerky broth for Peg.

The sky was beginning to streak with gray when the broth boiled. He killed the fire with water and removed the gag from her mouth. Untying her so he could prop her to a sitting position, he forced her to drink.

St. Clair needed sleep but feared to trust Peg unattended, so he retied and gagged her when the broth was gone. He had no way of knowing whether or not the Sioux would return, but if anyone should hear her call out, he would be in a hopeless position to defend her.

He slept throughout the morning and when he awoke it was without the gentle transition from slumber to wakefulness. Peg Delaney was asleep, her face wet with perspiration. St. Clair leaned against the wall, suddenly weak with relief.

A careful reconnaissance from all sides of the boat revealed no sign of the enemy;

he could not have felt more alone on an alien planet. Sergeant Royce's packet was nowhere in sight and no Indians were in view.

St. Clair broke up the little three-legged stool and kindled a small fire to heat another canteen of broth. He ate some biscuits and jerky, then untied Peg and tried to awaken her. She groaned and pushed him away, but her cheeks were cool and he knew that the fever had broken. He shook her. She opened her eyes, then sat up slowly.

"I fixed you something to eat," he said. "The Missouri River blue-plate."

"I think I'm going to be sick," she said. She tried to stand but fell to her knees. He lifted her up and helped her outside. When she felt better he led her back into the cabin again and she sipped the broth. After she finished, she sat hunched over, her arms around her upraised knees. Perspiration beaded her forehead and glistened on her cheeks. Finally she said, "I've been a real mess, haven't I?"

He smiled. "Have you heard me complain?"

"You wouldn't," she said. She looked down at her shirt and yellow-striped soldier pants. "There isn't much about me

136

that you don't know now, is there?"

"I still don't know who Jim is," he said, and at her shocked expression was sorry that he had been so stupid. He hurried on to an explanation. "You were delirious last night. You mentioned 'Jim.' Forget it."

"What did I say?"

He realized later that he should have answered her, invented some triviality, but from his silence she drew a story and believed that her words had been too indelicate to repeat.

"I — guess I owe you an explanation," she said softly.

"You don't owe me anything," he said uncomfortably. "I told you to forget it."

"I see," she said, and tipped her head down, studying the grain of the wood under her feet. "Now I know what I must have said."

He stood up and touched the top of her head with his hand before turning away to gather their meager equipment. The rucksack of food went on his back, the roll of blankets over his shoulder. He carried the rifle in the sling position and the Dragoon pistol nestled beneath his left armpit.

"We'll have to leave now," he told her. "Buckley has wounded with him and he'll go slow. I think we can catch him." He remembered then that she had no shoes and stopped to wrap her feet with blanket strips.

She was very weak and he had to help her onto the improvised raft before pushing toward shore. As soon as they reached dry ground, he set their course following Buckley's command.

St. Clair was forced to hold down his speed, for Peg could scarcely walk a mile without resting. All that afternoon they pushed their way through country that was rolling and generally open. Having no compass to guide him, he stayed near the river where they also had some brush and trees to screen them.

By early evening he realized they had covered only half the distance he had hoped for. He kept this disappointment to himself, but Peg realized that she was holding him back. Regret showed in her eyes.

Buckley left a clear trail; he could not avoid it. The marks left by the travois were deep scars in the soft earth. St. Clair and the girl kept on until twilight, then scanned the land for a possible resting place. He chose a deep cutbank where brush gave fair cover from three sides. From a military standpoint this would be difficult to de-

fend, but it offered the maximum conceal-
ment for a fire, which Peg Delaney needed
badly.

Putting his equipment aside, St. Clair
dug with his knife into the soft earth face
of the bank until he had a hollow indented
about three feet square. This he braced
with crossed branches and one stout pole.

He kindled a fire near the mouth and
spread the blankets for Peg. The meal was
beef jerky on pointed green sticks. The biscuits had hardened, and had to be broken
with the butt of his pistol, then soaked in
water before they could be eaten.

As soon as the meal was finished, St.
Clair stamped out the fire and sat in silence while a full darkness descended. He
brushed his hand against his cheek and his
whiskers whispered. Fatigue sketched lines
around his eyes and lent a pinched look to
his lips.

From the blankets Peg said, "Quincy, get
some sleep."

"Later."

"Now," she insisted. He turned his head
and looked at her, barely able to see her in
the dim light. St. Clair sighed and pulled
off his boots before lying down beside her.
She shivered and moved closer to him and
he put his arm around her waist. He could

feel her breasts against his chest and suddenly the complexion of this adventure changed.

He may have stiffened slightly for he transmitted this feeling to her in some way and she put a hand on his shoulder, asking, "What?"

"Nothing," St. Clair said evenly. "Go to sleep."

"I'm dead tired for a fact," she said, "but I can't sleep." She turned her head so that her breath fanned warmly on his cheek. He kept his hand, which was in the small of her back, absolutely motionless, and this reminded him of the agony of dancing school when he was eleven.

He recalled how acute his awareness of girls had been at that age; he loathed them vocally while his heart held a secret yearning. His dancing teacher had only vaguely understood and despaired when he insisted on holding his partner at extreme arm's length. Any closer proximity had been unendurable.

He smiled inwardly at the memory but still couldn't relax, and Peg, feeling this restraint, interpreted it as dislike for her. Her pride moved her slightly away from him and she said, "I'm sorry. You want to be alone."

Like lovers leaving incoherent gaps in their speech, yet ultimately understanding each other's desires, they reached a simultaneous conclusion. "Peg," he said softly, and yet his voice said more for she was in a state of mind to receive the full import of what he wanted to say.

Quickly she turned back, reaching for him as he reached for her. And then she was searching in the darkness for his lips, her own warm with promise and invitation. The pressure of his arms hurt her and yet she welcomed the hurt.

He pulled his lips away finally and concentrated on beating down the white heat of emotion that threatened to overwhelm him. By sheer will alone he forced himself into objectivity, then further separated himself from her.

This time she understood, realizing what he was doing, yet knowing how he needed her. She said, "Why do we lie to each other? There'll never be a tomorrow for us. Can't we just take this hour?"

He was sober now; the wine of passion drained away. "You're wrong," he told her. "There *will* be a tomorrow, and how will we think of it then, Peg? What will we say?"

"We won't speak of it," she said evenly.

141

"There won't be any regrets, Quincy. Ever."

"We're desperate now," he told her softly. "People should never do anything when they're desperate."

A new rapport flowed between them and he realized why she had offered him her love. With a woman's compassion she had felt his momentary insecurity in the precariousness of their position and believing all hope gone had offered what comfort she could. He saw this clearly and he found that he could now touch her without flame. He cupped her face tenderly between his palms and kissed her lips, her cheeks, her eyes. She clung to him tightly, aware of his refusal, yet knowing that she had taken on a deeper meaning for him.

She lay back and he tucked the blanket up under her chin.

"Don't go," she said.

"I must," he said softly, and brushed the hair away from her forehead. There was a new intimacy in the touch of his hands. She had invited it and was glad. Hereafter whenever their eyes met, their hands touched, each would remember this night and what it might have been.

"I'm going along the river for a look around," he said and handed her the .44 Dragoon Colt. "Can you use that?"

"I'll be all right," she assured him and he moved away like a shadow through the brush. She cuddled the heavy revolver against her chest. It was still warm from the protection of his arm.

St. Clair paused on the river bank. There was a sliver of moon, enough to throw an oily sheen on the water. A breeze stirred the leaves of the tree over him and he sat down, his legs crossed, the carbine in his lap.

For half an hour he remained motionless, then moved his head when he heard a muffled beat of sound downstream. For a brief time he couldn't identify it, even though it was familiar. Then he understood what he was hearing. The stolen packet with Sergeant Royce in command was slowly pushing upstream against the current.

The sound of the steam engine grew louder and he could now hear the thump of the paddlewheel shafts. He stood up and leaned out and then saw the low, dark shape rounding a bend.

St. Clair turned and hurried through the brush. When he reached their camp, he found Peg sitting up in the blankets.

"What is it?"

"Royce and the packet," he said and

began to make up his pack. She got off the blankets and rolled them for him and was waiting when he shouldered the plunder. He took the pistol from her and tucked it in the spring holster.

"I'm only guessing," he said, "but Royce must be trying to get ahead of Buckley and the column. There must be a crossing somewhere above and Royce is going to stop Buckley there."

She touched him lightly on the chest. "Quincy, go on and leave me. I'm holding you back."

"We'll go together," he said. "It won't be easy because we'll have to push for all we're worth. But we can catch Buckley. We've got to, Peg."

CHAPTER 7

"I think," Lieutenant Buckley said to Sergeant Delaney, "we've passed the crossing."

The column had halted and men lay in exhausted immobility on the ground. The horses stood with heads drooping and the sharp flavor of nitrogen mingled with man odors and the sweetness of chewing tobacco on the night breeze. Here and there a wounded man moaned and a voice would say soothingly, "Easy now, Mac. One more to go to make corporal. One more, Mac."

"We must have passed the crossing," Lieutenant Buckley said, irritated because his maps were a soggy pulp. "Pass the word back. Rest for fifteen minutes then backtrack."

"Yes, sor," Delaney said, and walked down the length of the column.

Buckley surveyed his command with dull, defeated eyes. He raised one hand and scrubbed it across his face. The sight of the ill-equipped troopers, the gentle lament of the wounded, shook the foundations of his faith and in that moment hope fled.

Lieutenant McAuliff came up, saluted and said, "Sir, we need a surgeon. I have four fractures — three that need probing —"

"Mister, we have no surgeon." Whatever defeat his mind acknowledged, he kept from his voice. "Do the best you can. They're soldiers. They'll have to take a soldier's chances."

Lieutenant McAuliff walked away with weary steps and Jules Buckley sat down, his long legs tucked under him. For hours now he had been forcing his mind away from thoughts of Peg Delaney and Quincy St. Clair, but in this moment of tired relaxation the nagging doubts crowded him and he was forced to face them squarely.

He now held no hope for either of them.

Buckley could not summon the proper emotion in regard to St. Clair. The man wasn't an old friend, so there could be no real grief. Neither was he a stranger meriting little more than passing sympathy. Buckley couldn't pin down the regret in his mind, either to the fact that he had lost an undercover agent, or a potentially fine officer.

He tried not to think at all about Peg Delaney.

He'd thought about her too much already.

He wondered how any sane, sensible man could remain in love with a girl who regarded him in the same category as a brother. In the year 1848, his first assignment as a junior officer had been to the cavalry troop protecting the engineers who built Fort Kearney. Nine years ago. He wondered where the time had gone. Peg had been eleven then, motherless, and thus allowed to accompany her father. Counting the commandant's wife, there had been eight women at Kearney, but of all he remembered Peg best, Peg with her pigtails, too-large eyes filled with warm regard for him, and her unabashed attachment to him.

That had been four years before Jim graduated, he recalled. The thought brought wrinkles to his forehead. Remembering suddenly placed a new focus on the whole affair and Buckley discovered facts in his brother that had previously escaped him. *I was always the big brother to her,* Buckley decided, *while Jim was cast in the role of lover from the very beginning.*

Jim bad been dashing, and very young and handsome, while Jules was already beginning to don the cloak of eternal sternness that marked the efficient cavalry officer.

She needed laughter and Jim gave it to her, he thought. *I suppose that's why I'm so critical of St. Clair. He has Jim's recklessness.*

Buckley picked up a handful of leafmold and sifted it through his fingers. At fifteen a girl is standing on the threshold of womanhood and every experience is an adventure. Looking back, he could see that he had blamed Jim Buckley unjustly. No man could have resisted Peg Delaney.

For a little over a year he had broiled in the cauldron of his own emotions while his brother wooed the girl he loved. Then it ended abruptly; in one moment of agony the finish had been written.

During the building of Fort Riley in 1853, the Indians had been particularly bothersome and Lieutenant James Buckley had been too daring. A contact, a swift pursuit, a grim moment when men strained together, eyes glazed, muscles overtaxed — and four men out of a patrol of twelve escaped with their lives. The next day another patrol brought back the remains, one hand and one foot hacked off of each corpse, hair a crimson ruin.

Jules Buckley clearly recalled the events that followed. He made one clumsy effort to swing from the role of brother to that of lover but his reception had been so indifferent that he never again dared to make such an attempt. From that day on Peg made it a point never to speak of Jim. And thereafter he saw her differently, more mature than her years allowed, more wise than she had a right to be.

Their relationship was painfully friendly, nothing more.

"Pardon me, sir. We're ready to move out."

Jules Buckley raised his eyes and found Lieutenant McAuliff standing there. He had not heard the man approach.

"Pass the word back then," Buckley said, and slowly pushed himself erect.

For over an hour Quincy St. Clair had maintained a wearisome pace, but at last he stopped when Peg Delaney fell and could not get up. They were in a small clearing of tall grass not far from the river bank. The night carried a damp chill and they huddled together, their breathing labored and rapid.

"I'm all right," Peg said at last, but she leaned on St. Clair when she stood up.

There was no sign of the packet. Sergeant Royce had steamed on upstream and the fact that St. Clair had no way of knowing what the man planned sawed at his nerves. He put an arm around Peg and helped her across the clearing, then paused as soon as there was timber and screening brush around them.

The moonlight seemed stronger now, casting an even grayness over the land and transforming the river into a twisted silver ribbon. St. Clair made an attempt to orient himself and found it difficult. The land near the river was moderately hilly but soon flattened into a near plain. In his native New York State, mountains rose in a predictable fashion and a man soon learned to follow the natural ruptures. But here, he feared to leave the river because he felt sure that once in the open, his sense of direction would desert him.

He was considering these things when Peg touched him on the arm, drawing his attention around and across the three-quarter mile clearing. At first he saw nothing. Then a shadow shifted unnaturally, and another, and he felt a quick clutch of fear.

For several minutes he watched. Two of the men he recognized as soldiers; the other three were Indians and he had seen enough in the last twenty-four hours to recognize them as Sioux. The Indians were scouting in the lead while the two soldiers, armed with carbines, brought up the rear.

"They're after us," he whispered. His first thought was to run for it, yet something held him. Without analyzing it, he was learning how to become a frontiersman. The Indians were tracking in poor light and he knew that the hard imprint of his cavalry boots was beckoning them on.

He was a soldier and his military mind told him that the odds were too great. Strategy was his only defense here and if he had to take desperate measures the occasion justified it. The familiar wind of rashness swayed him and he smiled. Here was a game he enjoyed and he found the invitation irresistible.

"I don't think they know you're with me," he said softly. He pointed to the cloth wrappings on her feet. "You're not leaving the tracks I am." He glanced around, then led her to a thicket twenty yards distant. "Stay here," he said, but she grabbed his arm and held him.

"You're going to do something foolish for me," she said. "Please don't."

"I'm going to do something foolish because that's the way I am," he told her. "Peg, I can't make a stand — I'd never get

151

all of them. I'm going to try a trick, and if it comes off I'll be back for you. If I don't succeed then you'll be no worse off than if I were killed here." He handed her the carbine. "There's one shot there, Peg. Do you know what to do with it?"

"Shoot me an Indian," she said. Her hand caressed his unshaven cheek in a gesture of farewell, and then he bent low and slipped through the dense brush.

Instantly he was aware of being alone and the feeling of abandonment shocked him. He understood then why mountain men liked dogs; they helped to dispel the complete isolation.

His only experience as a woodsman had been deer hunting in the Adirondacks, but it was enough to master the rudiments of stalking. *Deer or men,* he thought, *what's the difference?*

Thirty yards from the thicket that sheltered Peg Delaney, he pushed boldly into the grass, the .44 Dragoon Colt clutched in his fist. Moving along on his hands and knees, he kept his head low and wormed toward the men who were now a third of the way across the clearing.

The Indians were still in the lead and St. Clair turned his head to look back. The brush and woods were a black, undefined mass fifty yards to his rear. He tucked the Colt beneath his arm to cock it lest he warn the sharp-eared Sioux.

His patience amazed him. The Indians paused once and gestured while the soldiers hurried up. One of the Sioux, a tall warrior in beaded buckskins, pointed toward the dark foliage across the clearing.

St. Clair raised himself on one elbow to sight along the barrel of his revolver. The distance was forty yards, but the Indians were moving again and the range dwindled rapidly. He waited, holding the silver front sight squarely on the Sioux's breastbone. When the range narrowed to twenty yards, he touched off the .44.

Flame and smoke erupted and the gun recoiled violently, but the Indian wheeled half around and fell heavily. One of the soldiers whipped up his carbine and shot too quickly. The bullet snipped grass a yard from St. Clair's elbow. Re-cocking, St. Clair drove a steady shot at the man and watched him collapse while the two remaining Sioux went belly-flat into the grass. The soldier who had been hit tried to drag himself forward while St. Clair scooted away to a new position.

The remaining soldier stood flat-footed and fired his carbine at nothing, reloaded and fired again. St. Clair drew a bead on the man and speculated whether or not to shoot him. His worry concentrated on the two Sioux. They were worth ten soldiers in this kind of fight.

St. Clair shot the remaining soldier in the chest and moved again.

Secure for the moment, he lay motionless and waited. He heard no sounds at all save the wind brushing the grass. While he waited he broke open a box of paper cartridges and crushed three into the cylinder with the ramrod. He capped the nipples and cocked the gun, then tried to beat down a rising panic. *This is your game,* he reminded himself. *This is the way you like to play, wild and close with the stakes high.*

No man could long hold his edge in battle, he decided. His first success had been due to surprise and he had accounted for three of the enemy, but now he realized that he should have shot the Indians instead of wasting his bullets on the soldiers.

A few minutes ago he had blessed the night wind that rustled the grass. Then it had screened his approach, but now it shielded the enemy. The paradox galled him.

He decided to move again.

In a new position twenty yards to the left

of the old, he lay flat, breathing through his open mouth. He speculated on the wisdom of attempting to reach the edge of the brush, discarding this idea when he realized how outclassed he would be in woods fighting.

Daring ideas often shock the men who conceive them and St. Clair found this so as he lay motionless, stunned by the boldness of the plan that had leaped into his mind. He toyed with this scheme like a man fondling a petard, with awe, gingerly, lest it explode. But the more he considered it, the less hare-brained it seemed.

At least it offered a two to one chance, and a fight on his own terms.

With this decision, he leaped to his feet in clear view, his Dragoon pistol ready. He had to wait no more than a second for results. Ten yards to his right a head raised, then shoulders, and the long barrel of a trade musket swept toward him. St. Clair stood his ground as cool and precise as if he were at the pistol butts firing for troop record. Breath! Hold it! Squeeze! His shot struck the Sioux in the jaw and carried away part of his head.

"Now we're even," St. Clair said as he whipped his head around to locate the other Indian. His nerves were tight wire as he squinted, trying to pierce the night. He saw a shadow rise up from the grass and shot at it, knowing instinctively that he had been over-anxious and would miss. The Sioux was sprinting for the brush. He whirled once to fire his musket at St. Clair. The ball passed overhead.

Throwing down the musket, the Sioux made a plunging dive for the dark foliage. St. Clair followed, knowing as he did that he was taking too great a chance. As he ran through the grass he could hear the movement ahead of him and let his ears guide him. The night wind distorted the sound slightly and led him astray, but there was nothing confusing about Peg Delaney's scream.

He altered his course abruptly and charged through the brush, smashing it down with the force of his momentum. Branches tore his clothes and whipped him across the chest. The boom of Peg's carbine was a deep slap, like a retreat howitzer loaded with wad and powder. A yell lifted, but it was the Indian who cried out.

St. Clair ground to a halt and listened. Ahead, brush crackled like wrinkled paper and the Sioux hove into view, staggering as he ran. St. Clair raised his pistol and fired at the dodging brave and missed.

He did not follow. The sudden release from the fight left him tired and strained. He turned and tried to identify the clump of bushes where he had left Peg, but he had approached from a different angle and it all looked strange.

When he heard her soft voice call, "Quincy?" he smiled with relief, then walked directly to her hiding place.

She still clutched the fired carbine.

"I missed him," she said, and began to tremble.

He reloaded his .44 pistol and tucked it in the spring holster beneath his arm. Then he reloaded the carbine for her. By this time Peg had regained her composure somewhat. She said, "If a trooper did what you just did, you'd upbraid him for it. I knew another like you once. He died young."

"The question is, did he die happy?" he asked quietly. He laughed then, for his nerves had calmed. "That *was* a stupid thing to do, wasn't it?"

"Were they from the packet?"

"I suppose so," St. Clair said. "Royce must have put them ashore below the wrecks and told them to scout around. They must have found where Buckley marched out and followed him. I'd say that the Sioux who were tracking found my footprints and got curious."

"Where do you think the packet is now?"

"I don't know." He massaged the back of his neck. There was a dull ache at the base of his skull and his eyes burned intensely. "Upstream somewhere. I hope he's far enough from here that he didn't hear the shooting."

"Royce must intend to tie up someplace along the river," Peg said. "He'd pick up his soldiers wouldn't he?"

"Probably at the crossing," St. Clair said. He swung his head to look in both directions, worrying about the Sioux who had got away, wondering how badly he was hurt. If he ever reached Royce . . . "We'd better go on," he said, and shouldered the carbine and blankets.

As they started along the river again, St. Clair realized that he had lost his fear of this country. The discovery was mildly surprising until he recalled the fashion in which he had been 'blooded.' He had fulfilled his function as a soldier, to stand and deliver, to face the enemy on his own terms and defeat him.

This was far different from the shooting of Rance Ranier. He felt rather than saw the contrast. From this fight he had learned the right lessons and they filled him with confidence, validated the boldness that so often had carried him into trouble.

St. Clair considered the Sioux who had been tracking for Royce's soldiers. What manner of sign had they read on the ground? He began to observe more details along the river and swung his head frequently from side to side. This increased vigilance was rewarded not ten minutes later when he found a trooper's yellow handkerchief.

He had to pause once to retie the cloth 'boots' Peg Delaney wore. She was very tired. New lines of strain showed in her face, but she dredged up a smile for him.

"We're still on Buckley's trail," he assured her, and started off again. Later he began to discover other clues, smashed grass, a scuff in the earth where a leather heel had scarred it, the white shards of a broken branch where a trooper had knocked it from his path.

Putting all of these small things together, he found that Buckley's patrol was leaving a wide trail, a trail easily followed.

From behind him, Peg asked, "Do you think we're catching up with the column?"

"I don't know," he admitted. "Surely

they can't be more than four hours ahead of us."

He paused to let her rest again and leaned his back against hers so she could brace herself to massage her legs. Her hair was tangled and matted with bits of bark and leaves. Mosquitoes pestered them with their whine and sting.

Peg sighed. "I'd give anything for a bit of soap."

He became aware of his own odor, the gaminess of five days unwashed. His beard itched and the sweat on his cheeks added to his discomfort.

He sat quietly until he judged half an hour had passed, then pulled Peg to her feet. She groaned as she forced aching muscles into movement. His heart wrenched with pity for her but he could do nothing to ease their condition. When he moved out again, she stayed one pace behind.

CHAPTER 8

For the remainder of the night, St. Clair did not permit himself to linger more than five minutes during each rest stop. An hour before dawn they paused at the edge of a willow thicket. The moon was hours dead and the pre-dawn dark was thick, but he could make out the blocky shape of the packet moored on a sandbar in mid-stream.

Peg crowded close to him and asked, "What does it mean, Quincy? Why would Royce stop here?"

"I'm not sure, but this could be the crossing," he said. He leaned on the barrel of the carbine and studied the land on both sides of the river. The shores were flat here, almost forming a beach on each side.

Timber grew within thirty yards of the water's edge and the brush was thick, but only waist high. "Wait here," he said, and handed her the carbine as she sat down. He edged away and searched the ground for some sign of Buckley's crossing, but could find nothing to indicate that the column had been through here.

He saw scars in the earth leading to the west and after another twenty minutes of careful search, reached the conclusion that Buckley must have continued on.

He's sure to realize he missed it, St. Clair thought, and back-tracked to where Peg Delaney rested.

He found her asleep and unrolled a blanket to spread over her. Then he squatted in the fringe of the brush and studied the packet. There was no evidence of life aboard and yet he felt confident that Royce and his soldiers were there. The sergeant was not a fool. He would never risk losing the packet by bivouacking his men ashore.

Laboriously the sky lightened and then he heard the first muted sounds of movement drift across the water. A door closed heavily on the Texas deck and a man's boots rattled on the companionway. A moment later someone spoke in a rough voice. Within a few minutes, Royce had his troop awake and eating their cold rations.

In his mind, St. Clair tried to follow Royce's reasoning. Obviously the sergeant intended to deny Buckley the use of the ford, but how could Royce be so positive that Buckley would try to cross here?

Then the answer came chime clear and

the pieces of the puzzle fell gently into place. Royce had steamed carefully upstream with the Sioux scouting ahead. Possibly a report had come back that Buckley had missed the crossing and turned his column back.

That had to be it.

Royce's men aboard the packet wouldn't present too formidable a force against Buckley, but Royce was hiding his ace, the Sioux. St. Clair waited until the light grew stronger and a grayness filled the land. He looked searchingly across the reach of river at the opposite bank but could see nothing.

You won't see them until they attack. . . .

The Sioux were there; he was willing to gamble on it. Royce would not fight on equal terms. He would only fight when he outnumbered Buckley five to one, and he did when a man counted the Indians.

Peg stirred and St. Clair put his hand on her arm, bringing her eyes wide open. She sat up, groaning slightly as she moved. He draped the blanket around her shoulders and she hunched over for warmth.

"No sign of Buckley," he said, "but he's coming back this way." He explained his reasoning. "That sergeant is a smart tactician. He's pretending to be a sitting duck and Buckley will see him there, measure him, then attack. Only it's not going to work that way, Peg. Buckley's going to get his men floundering in midstream and then that whole shore over there is going to turn into Sioux. Buckley will be caught in a place he can't get out of."

"Can't we do something?"

"I don't know what," he said, and turned gloomily to study the land in the first rays of the new sun. The distance between their hiding place and the beached packet might exceed three hundred yards. The river was very wide here and there was no cover at all when one neared the beach. Buckley would have his entire column in clear view of Royce before the head of the column ever touched water. Once started, there would be no stopping. To turn back under fire was unthinkable.

Peg Delaney heard the sounds first, simply because she was so near complete exhaustion that her senses had been acutely sharpened. She gripped St. Clair's arm and then he too heard it — the shuffle of booted feet, the rattle of bit chains, the knock of carbine stock against canteen.

He judged the column to be no more than a quarter mile away.

St. Clair turned his eyes back to the packet moored on the sandbar. Men were moving about the lower deck and upon the Texas. The wheelhouse door opened and Sergeant Royce stepped out with another man. St. Clair recognized Royce in spite of the distance.

He knew that the mutinous sergeant had heard Buckley's approaching column and St. Clair found himself in a position to view a great tragedy with no apparent way to prevent it. Royce was deliberately exposing himself to entice Buckley into battle, and after what Royce had already done to the command, Buckley would hardly let this offer go unchallenged.

St. Clair recognized the physical impossibility of trying to intercept Buckley. And he certainly could not hope to defeat Royce single-handed.

Desperation often breeds inspiration and St. Clair again estimated the distance between himself and the packet. A good three hundred yards, he decided, and bellied down in the fringe of their cover.

Royce was still standing by the wheelhouse. St. Clair took a careful prone position, cocking his carbine. He elevated the rear sight, centered the front blade on Sergeant Royce's chest, let his breath out and squeezed the trigger.

The recoil rammed him back and

powder smoke obscured the packet. Someone yelled and men began to mill around on the deck. The smoke dissipated and St. Clair saw that a man was down. But a more careful study told him that his windage had been off. He had hit the man standing next to Royce.

But the calculated shot had been sufficient. Listening again, St. Clair could no longer hear the crunch of Buckley's approaching command. Whatever advantage Sergeant Royce had had was now lost. The hidden Sioux across the river mistook the shot for a signal and spilled out onto the far beach, shouting, screaming and firing their trade muskets.

Lieutenant Buckley came on, his column fanning out for skirmishing and fully aware of the military situation. At the far end of the line a few carbines rattled and several Sioux cascaded from their horses as they rode into the water on the far side.

Aboard the packet, Royce was furiously shouting orders. His men began to fire at the small blooms of powder smoke along the shore, but they did little damage. St. Clair could see that Sergeant Royce longed to launch his troopers in an attack, but he dared not for fear of having his men picked off in the waist-deep water. He was committed to the sandbar. He had to remain there to support the Sioux who were now pushing their premature attack.

Buckley had the edge with his sharpshooters. The Indians tried twice to breach the crossing but the horses floundered in the water and troopers picked them off with a withering fire. Nearly halfway across, they broke their charge to mill about, then faded toward the far bank and cover.

Barricaded on the packet, Royce's men put up a stiff fight but Buckley's men were firing from concealed positions and moving after each shot. Royce's carbine fire slashed the brush and inflicted a few casualties, but on the whole was futile in effect.

St. Clair and the girl worked their way into deeper brush and came upon Lieutenant Buckley's position from the rear. Overriding the snapping rattle of carbine fire, the commanding voice of the C horn pinpointed the command post, for where the bugler is, so is the commanding officer.

On the opposite shore, the Sioux were massing for another attempt to breast the river, and Corporal McLairnan took six men to work his way a hundred yards upstream to a new position. From behind a waterlogged tree they began to fire, two at a time, and the Sioux braves felt the telling effect.

Warriors fell from their horses and the Sioux became disorganized, frantically churning the water and screaming. They fired their muskets but the distance was great and their aim bad. After ten minutes of this, Corporal McLairnan withdrew his men and rejoined the main body, for the Sioux had obviously lost heart.

Royce kept on fighting, but the men on shore were taking a toll aboard the packet. Five dead men could be seen draped half over the side of the lower deck. The wheelhouse was a shambles and the men there had circled it to take cover on the other side. Royce stood on the Texas, shouting orders that were unintelligible in the fury of battle.

Pausing in a thicket, St. Clair parted the foliage and nearly stepped on a soldier. The man wheeled, his carbine ready, then sat up. Jim Overmile's face showed shocked surprise. He said, "Sufferin' saints! Is that you?"

"A little worse for wear." St. Clair nodded toward his right. "Lieutenant Buckley over there?"

"Fifteen, twenty yards up," Overmile said, and grinned.

St. Clair put his arm around Peg and pushed the brush aside for her with the barrel of his carbine. In a very soft voice Peg was repeating, "I won't cry I won't cry I just won't."

Sergeant Delaney flipped his head around when he heard the brush snap. He saw his daughter and he put down his carbine carefully and stood up. He looked very old and badly worn. Tears spilled over his bottom lids and washed runnels in the dirt on his cheeks. He put his arms around Peg and Buckley turned as though pulled by some metaphysical force.

St. Clair saluted and said, "Trooper St. Clair reporting to the command, sir." He smiled. "We were unavoidably detained."

Someone yelled and the sound of firing slackened.

Peering through the brush, St. Clair saw Royce backing the packet off the sandbar and edging his way down stream to turn around.

"The dirty son's runnin' out again!" someone yelled.

"Aim for the paddlewheels! Aim for the paddlewheels!"

"What good will that do?"

"Fire by volley, dammit! Fire by volley!"

Lieutenant Buckley turned to his trumpeter. "Sound 'cease fire.'"

The tones of the horn split the shouting and shooting like a knife through warm cheese and the clamor fell off, leaving only the muttered cursing of the disappointed.

The aftermath of any fight is a space in time when confusion grips men and they grope blindly for some remembered sense of reality. Nerves began to let go and troopers huddled together in mute groups, just sitting. Someone produced a plug of tobacco and passed it around. Then another began to clean his carbine. *Misery loves company,* St. Clair thought, then turned as Lieutenant Buckley touched him.

Sergeant Delaney posted guards. Troopers fronted the river in case another attack developed. The bulk of the command remained screened by the brush. A detail was dispatched for the horses and litter wounded who had been left a hundred yards behind with a small guard.

Out of earshot of the troop, Buckley stripped off his gauntlets and wiped one hand across his face. "St. Clair, I'd given you up for dead. I expected you to rejoin the column no later than yesterday." He inclined his head toward the river. "You fire that first shot?"

"Yes, sir," St. Clair said.

"Dammit, man," Buckley said, "I don't know whether to put you on report or write you up in a dispatch." He wiped his hand across his face again and glanced over his shoulder. Buckley found himself in the uncomfortable position of having to act calm when he didn't feel that way at all. He wanted to rush to Peg Delaney, to embrace her and make a damned fool of himself and he knew that he couldn't. She wouldn't want that.

St. Clair made his report briefly, covering the pertinent details of their escape. He spoke of the five men who had been following the column. "Royce must have put them ashore a few miles below the camp in the hope that they'd contact you before you returned here. Fortunately, I ran into them first."

Buckley's face was stern. "In that moment of insanity when you decided to fight five-to-one odds, I don't suppose it occurred to you that you were gambling with Peg Delaney's life. No, I can see that it didn't. All right, we're still in trouble. Lieutenant McAuliff is taking a nose check now, but we've sustained casualties in this rondelay, no mistake. Casualties I can't afford to have."

171

Brush crackled behind them and Lieutenant McAuliff came up, one arm dangling uselessly. Blood dripped from his fingertips and his face was gray with shock and pain.

"What the devil is this?" Buckley demanded. "Get that taken care of, Mister. If you don't give a damn for yourself, think of the investment the government has in you."

McAuliff rendered a left-handed salute. "Reporting, sir. Two dead and one wounded slightly. We're in good shape, sir."

"We're in lousy shape," Buckley said irritably. "Get Sergeant Delaney to patch that arm. That's an order, Mister!"

"Yes, sir," McAuliff said, and went away.

Buckley shook his head sadly. "He thinks he bobbled on the packet and he'll get himself killed trying to make it up. A damn shame. He's in your school, St. Clair. The book is fine to go by when it conforms with his theories. When it doesn't, he throws it away."

"May I make a suggestion, sir?"

Buckley raised his eyes to St. Clair. "You've been trained as an officer and right now I'm ready to listen to anything, political speeches included."

"I was thinking that without enough mounts and the wounded to slow us, we'll have a tough time making the march, sir. What I'm trying to say is: Sergeant Royce meant to deny us this crossing and we beat him back. Since the entire command is in no condition to march, why don't we wade out to the island, dig in, and prevent him from going upstream?"

Buckley's eyes were thoughtful. "It just might work. I'll split the command. One half to remain on this side of the crossing where the channel is, and the other half dug in on the island. We'll deny this crossing to the rebels and wait here for reenforcements. I'll get a runner off now."

He turned then and bawled, "Trumpeter! On the double here!"

CHAPTER 9

Troopers Carmichael, Doolin, and Rafferty volunteered to carry Lieutenant Buckley's message through the hostile country. They were allotted extra rations and surrendered their carbines for revolving pistols with a double supply of ammunition.

When Sergeant Delaney reported them ready, the three men were summoned to Buckley's command post to receive instructions.

"You will leave an hour apart. Rafferty, you go first. You follow him, Carmichael. Then Doolin. Men, I need not tell you how imperative it is that you get through. I hope you all make it, but the odds are against that. At Kansas City you will meet Captain Ackerman. Inform him in detail of what has happened. Report our position and tell him we'll try to hold this point for fifteen days. After that, I'm afraid it won't matter whether he comes or not."

He shook hands with each of them. "Good luck now."

Rafferty went to the water's edge and

walked out until it was halfway between his hips and knees, then pushed forward and began swimming. Buckley's command watched as he battled the current to emerge on the other side.

The early morning sun was weak, and an almost solid layer of high, thin clouds blocked out all but a feeble warmth. After Rafferty entered the thickets lining the opposite bank, Buckley turned his attention to fortifications.

"Sergeant Delaney," he said, "Mister McAuliff is out of action. Take a detail of ten men and entrench along the bank so that the firepower commands this ford downstream. Then handpick a dozen men and wade out to the island. Establish fortifications there and take Trooper St. Clair with you."

McAuliff was lying on a blanket a few yards away and overheard this. He struggled to a sitting position, his injured arm in a tourniquet. "But, sir," he said, "I request permission to command the island forces."

"Permission denied," Buckley said, then realized his tone had been too brusque. He walked over to McAuliff and looked down at the unnatural pallor on his slender face. "Mr. McAuliff, I need you here. As your commander, I don't think it's necessary to explain my orders in detail. Is it?"

"Not at all, sir," McAuliff said. He sank back on the blanket, his breathing labored and rapid.

"Get on with it, Sergeant," Buckley said.

Delaney said in an aside, "The lieutenant's bad hurt, sor. He's out of steam and runnin' on pure guts. That tourniquet stopped the bleedin', but if it's kept on long, he'll lose the arm."

"I know," Buckley said softly, watching McAuliff writhe in pain. "Better get your men selected, Sergeant. St. Clair, I think we'd better agree now on a plan of action."

Buckley squatted and marked the ground with a stick. "The river goes into a long curve here, and the deepest channel is on this side of the island. Dig in good out there, and pour enough squad fire into that packet to make Royce think the whole damn command is on that island. Make it so hot for him that he'll haul in close to this bank to get by. We'll be waiting for him — and I want him close enough to shoot the bolts off the wheelhouse door."

"I'll put him in your pocket, sir," St. Clair promised.

"You'd better," Buckley said and walked away, already calling to another man. "Corporal McEvoy! Shoot one of those

176

quartermaster mules and butcher it. See that a squad fire is built far enough back so it won't show. I want a hot meal in every man within an hour and a half."

St. Clair sat down on the ground between two spindly bushes and rested his head and shoulders against an oak deadfall. He let himself go loose all over and the ache in his back and legs subsided. He closed his eyes and listened to the sounds around him. A pistol popped and he heard the mule fall heavily.

Someone approached him from behind and he was instantly alert, his hand stabbing toward his shoulder holster.

"Don't shoot," Peg Delaney said. "I'm on your side."

She settled beside him and gave him a tired smile. "Are you going out on the island with Pop?" He nodded. "I thought so, so I told him to take care of you. Now I'm asking you to take care of him." He sat with his head tipped forward, his chin almost touching his chest. When she gripped his arm, he raised up and looked at her. "Quincy," she said hesitantly, "about the other night — you understand how it was, don't you?"

"Yes," he said. "I understand."

"Thank you, Quincy." She stood up and

looked at him for a moment before adding, "I'm glad you didn't ask about Jim. I don't think I could have told you."

She left him and he sat there until Sergeant Delaney came up. "We're ready to move, lad. I've gathered the men — twelve tough ones who can shoot."

"All right," St. Clair said. He got to his feet, placed his hands on his hips and rotated his upper body to ease the stiffness.

Sergeant Delaney watched him. "What can a man say by way of thanks?"

"Don't say anything," St. Clair said, his lips lifting in a smile.

"You give the orders, boy," Delaney said solemnly, "and I'll follow 'em to hell."

St. Clair joined the twelve-man detail with Delaney, and for appearances sake, fell in to the right of the first rank, his carbine at trail-arms.

Delaney did not speak; there was nothing to say. These men knew their job and they followed him into the water, weapons and ammunition pouches held over their heads. They splashed across to the low island, where each man fell to digging with his knife. Within an hour the pits were dug in a shallow curve fronting the river channel, giving each man enough room to sit down. After completing the first trench, they dug another at right angles to form an L. With this type of protection, a trooper could defend an approach from either direction, swinging if attacked from either shore to another defensible position without having to expose himself.

For the rest of the morning the detail waited, hunkered down in their holes. There was no sign of the packet and to all appearances no Sioux within a hundred miles.

St. Clair slept while Sergeant Delaney watched. They had connecting trenches; this had been Delaney's idea. As far as the other troopers were concerned, St. Clair was just a soldier, a recruit, but Delaney never seemed to forget that he was an officer.

Delaney woke him near noon when two troopers pushed a small raft to the island with a bucket of hot stew. Two at a time, the men filled their mess cans and squatted to eat.

The mule meat was tough but when men have not had a hot meal in four days, such a small inconvenience can be overlooked. St. Clair cleaned up his plate of stew, then reassembled his meat can. With a full stomach he would have relished a cigar, but having none, he pushed the thought away. He settled down to sleep again and some time later a soldier from one of the other trenches whistled softly.

Thirteen heads raised cautiously until they saw the stolen packet rounding a far bend three hundred yards downstream. The vessel pushed ahead slowly. There were no Indian outriders along the banks.

St. Clair said, "Sergeant, pass the word: Let them close to one hundred yards and fire in volley — first squad, then second and third."

Delaney went to the end of the trench and spoke quietly. The word went around and men thrust the snouts of their carbines over the earth bulwarks. St. Clair watched breathlessly as the packet steamed closer. The freshly turned earth had been exposed to the sun long enough for it to dry and lose its dark color, so the mutineers on the packet's Texas did not spot the trenches until it was too late.

The packet was scarcely a hundred and fifty yards away when someone on the upper deck gave a shout and pointed. The paddlewheels stopped turning, then slowly began to reverse. But the packet was within range and St. Clair put a bullet through the pilothouse window, dropping the man at the helm.

Immediately the first squad raked the pilothouse in volley and one man crumpled while yet another slipped over the side, sending up a white splash when he hit the water. On the heels of this action, the second squad slammed lead into the men still on the Texas. One man dropped, clutching his leg, then dragged himself to safety as the third squad raked the fantail.

The first squad had rammed cartridges down the bore and recapped, firing as the packet stopped all forward motion and lay dead in the water. The pilothouse was unhealthy with this carbine fire, but Sergeant Royce made a desperate dash for the door and made it inside, crouching beneath the gaping window before anyone could draw a bead on him.

With the paddlewheels churning in reverse, the packet began to edge back, Royce blindly spinning the helm to head her into the shore. But as St. Clair had predicted, Sergeant Royce was not fool enough to run a packet head-on against entrenched riflemen. The man would try to make the channel close to the bank where his troopers could rake the pits with their fire.

Royce backed the packet to two hundred yards, then stopped the paddlewheels to churn forward, full steam ahead. The river boiled mud as the packet swung to the helm and St. Clair told Delaney to hold his fire until the packet drew abreast. Each man moved to the right-angle trench and waited.

Royce knew how helpless trench soldiers were when the enemy hit them from the flank and raked the trenches lengthwise, and he was hoping to do just that. He would call a good share of his men to the Texas where they could direct their fire downward.

As the packet came on, St. Clair nodded to Delaney and the old sergeant passed the word.

"Get ready to fire."

Buckley's troopers had not yet cracked a cap and their position remained unknown to Royce. He steamed boldly into the channel, bringing the packet alarmingly close to the shore. When he was nearly abreast, St. Clair nodded and the volley fire began. As he had expected, Royce had men lying flat on the Texas who began to fire back, but the angle trenches neutralized the crippling effect they had hoped for.

At that moment Buckley shattered their attempt to make the channel when he fired by squads and dumped half a dozen of Royce's men into the water. Bullets puckered the pilot house and shaved splinters from the decks while Royce viewed the hopelessness of his present position.

Once again the paddlewheels stopped and a moment later the packet was drifting in the channel. Too late, Royce realized his grave error. Bad as his position was, he would have been better off if he had braved the withering fire and gone through.

Now the packet lay inert while both forces laid a hail of crossfire upon it. Then slowly the paddlewheels reversed, frothing the water as the vessel edged back, staggered, it seemed, by the ferocity of the combined carbine fire.

Royce had less than a dozen men remaining in action and they took care not to expose themselves as the packet edged away. Buckley's men continued to pour lead on her, but she was backing well now, the current aiding in the withdrawal.

"Cease fire," St. Clair said quietly, and Sergeant Delaney passed the command. Buckley ended the shooting on the ringing notes of the trumpet and a sudden quiet descended over the river. Royce was near the bend now, while in the water dead men floated in the packet's wake.

"Perhaps we're no better off than before," St. Clair said to Delaney, "but we sure kept him from passing."

"The hard way," Delaney agreed.

The sergeant left the trench and moved around the small island to check for wounded. He found Jim Overmile squatting in his trench with a bloody forearm pinched between his fingers.

"Bad?" Delaney asked.

"Faith now," Overmile said, "had I a quart of good Irish whiskey, I'd be a new man."

"Pourin' whiskey in a wound can be dangerous," Delaney cautioned.

"Pour it?" Overmile's eyes widened in shock. "Man, I'd drink it!"

Buckley's trumpeter sounded officers' call and Delaney called to St. Clair, "Report to him, Trooper! I have pressin' duties here."

St. Clair laid aside his carbine and entered the water. He splashed across and found Buckley and Corporal McLairnan near the shore. "That'll be all, Corporal," Buckley said, and answered the man's salute.

The outcome of the fight had definitely raised Buckley's spirits. He gave St. Clair one of his rare smiles. "How did your detail fare?"

"Overmile slightly wounded, sir."

"They raked the brush pretty well on that last sweep," Buckley said. "I have three men down, one pretty bad." He walked down to the edge of the river and knelt to wash his face. When he came back to St. Clair water dripped from his goatee. "We'll have to go on short rations. Ammunition is low. Tell Delaney I want no promiscuous shooting." Buckley shot him a wry smile. "That was clever — digging the trenches in the shape of an L. Most young men who dream of the cavalry fail to master the infantry manual."

"Thank you, sir," St. Clair said, and encouraged by this rare praise, opened his mouth to speak again. Buckley cut him off with a wave of his hand.

"Save it. I want to remind you that our primary objective is to deny Royce the use of this channel. I intend to plug it against water transportation and move the command on. Our rations are low and the ammunition is getting too close. Take a dozen men and try falling logs into the channel. Given eight or ten hours I believe it could be blocked. At least enough to pin Royce where he is for a while."

"I was about to suggest that, sir," St. Clair said enthusiastically.

Buckley frowned. "Young man, I predict two things for you in regard to your future military career if you continue this impertinence with your superiors. Either you'll distinguish yourself and become a boy general, or you'll be drummed out of the corps for heresy, and the latter seems far more likely.

"Now, I would suggest that you collect as much waterlogged timber as you can find. The channel need not be dammed, just plugged sufficiently to allow no clearance."

"Very well, sir," St. Clair said stiffly. He saluted and returned to the island, smarting under the latest rebuke, but faithfully relaying the new plan to Sergeant Delaney. The detail was quickly organized and they began to scour the river bank for logs.

Once found, raising them became a problem that at first seemed insurmountable without the proper tools. St. Clair solved this after some careful thought by having the men fell half a dozen sturdy saplings. These were trimmed, leaving protruding knobs a foot long.

Good swimmers worked the ropes beneath the water soaked logs, then tied them to the knobs on the poles. Since the latter were nearly eighteen feet long and six inches in diameter, they supplied considerable buoyancy when rotated, a process that slowly windlassed the soaked logs off the bottom into a position where they could be mauled into the channel.

Until late afternoon the detail labored in chest deep water, striving to clog the channel. As the work progressed, interest quickened in those who watched from the shore and more men volunteered, pushing the mission ahead with increased speed until darkness fell.

CHAPTER 10

There was a pause for evening rations, then the work went on. Buckley waded out to the island to take a look. He found St. Clair on the edge of the beach, directing the lowering of a log.

"I can see," Buckley said, "that you studied the engineer's manual also. Given eight or nine years on the frontier, you might make a passable orderly." He smiled as he said this, his teeth flashing white in the pale moonlight. "Do you have the channel blocked yet?"

"No, sir," St. Clair admitted. "Far from it, I'm afraid. I judge that the packet will draw no more than two and a half feet of water, and there's still a four-foot head in the middle of the channel." He paused to think a moment. "If I could only devise a way to up-end the logs."

"I expect that our rebel sergeant will try another breakthrough tonight," Buckley said. "We'll have to be ready for him."

"Can we survive another attack, sir?"

"Not too well, but neither can he."

"Unless the Sioux reenforce him again, sir."

"I doubt they will," Buckley said. "I've been around Indians considerable, St. Clair, and I can tell you something about them. They make medicine and they believe in it. The trade muskets no doubt influenced the making of this particular medicine, but believe this, for it isn't in the manual and you can't learn it on the Plain: To fight Indians you have to be in force, or pretend that you will soon be supported by additional troops. It's necessary to frighten them until they stop thinking and retreat into their medicine. Then take that and turn *it* against them until they no longer have faith in it. Accomplish that and you've gone a long way toward defeating them."

"I still don't understand why they didn't return with Royce."

"Look at it this way," Buckley said patiently. "Royce was dealing with a race of people who trust no white man. When he enlisted their support, it was a half-hearted support at best. When we were first attacked, the advantage was theirs and they walked off the field counting coup. In their minds the medicine was strong — would win all battles. Their faith in Royce

189

mounted accordingly. But the next time you fired a shot and the edge was ours. The Sioux didn't win that battle. They had to turn tail, a thing that galls an Indian.

"So they began to doubt the medicine, and when Royce returned this morning he had to come alone. They were watching, and believe me, if Royce had broken through, their faith in his medicine would have been restored and we'd have been surrounded by howling fury."

"And now," St. Clair said, "you think they no longer trust him. Is that why you think they won't come back if he tries again?"

Buckley nodded. "That, coupled with the fact that no Sioux likes to fight at night. According to their beliefs, if a warrior is killed at night his soul wanders forever in darkness. A pretty grisly thought to an Indian. They like the dawn and a rise of ground with the sun behind them. A Sioux has only two tactics: The battle line where the warriors attack abreast, and the circle. Do anything to upset those two moves and you've rattled them."

"You should write a book, sir," St. Clair said.

"I think I'll wait until I know something," Buckley said dryly, and splashed back to shore.

By ten o'clock Trooper St. Clair knew that they could never succeed in blocking the channel in time, and he told Sergeant Delaney this. The sergeant ordered the troopers to abandon the project and they dragged themselves wearily upon the island, nearly waterlogged themselves.

St. Clair waded ashore and found Lieutenant Buckley alone. "I'm sorry, sir, but I don't think we've plugged it."

Buckley sighed. "Well, it was a good try anyhow. We can't have everything, can we?"

"No, sir," St. Clair said, then paused before adding, "If I might make a suggestion, sir —"

Lieutenant Buckley looked at him sharply. "St. Clair. I'm a tired man and very close to being a defeated one. Therefore I'm in no mood to consider your suggestions. I've been a soldier nine years and I like to fight my wars the old fashioned way. I suggest that you restrain yourself until you assume your own command. Then if your brilliant ideas get you into trouble, your own head will fall, not mine. Now return to the men on the island and we'll fight this one by the book."

St. Clair turned away without another word and returned to the island fuming inside. *Damned old woman, that's what he is! In a really stiff action, I'd probably have to eliminate him and take over for the good of the service. . . .*

A trooper saluted Lieutenant Buckley and said, "Sir, Lieutenant McAuliff's ravin', I'm sorry to say. That arm wound is worse, sir. He's runnin' one hell of a fever."

Buckley swore in a magnificently controlled manner. "That," he said, "reduces me to no officers, one sergeant and three corporals." He turned his head. "Sergeant Delaney, on the double here!"

The sergeant trotted up, came to attention and waited. "Sergeant, I don't suppose you're keeping a morning report."

Sergeant Delaney smiled. "In my head, sor. I'm a whiz at rememberin' details, sor."

"Lieutenant McAuliff is definitely out of action," Buckley said evenly, "and I'll need you here with me. I'm promoting Trooper St. Clair to sergeant, and Trooper Overmile to corporal. St. Clair can command the island detachment."

"Very good, sor," Delaney said, and dispatched a man to the island to carry the news.

Meanwhile St. Clair had decided upon a

192

course of action that he was positive would bring results and prove his worth to Lieutenant Buckley, once and for all. Therefore, when the man waded ashore to tell him of his promotion, St. Clair felt a secret elation. Buckley had unwittingly played right into his hand.

Immediately he set about the task of outlining his plan to the other men.

"Tonight, when the packet attacks, we're going to board her. You four men take the larboard side. Overmile, you're in charge of that detail. Board as near the paddlewheels as you can, but not too close. I understand they create a suction that will pull a man under. The rest of you come with me. We'll board on the starboard side and hit the wheelhouse. Our object is to get control of the helm and run her aground. I don't think I have to tell you to shoot for record."

There were no questions and the men returned to the trenches to get some rest. Overmile and St. Clair settled down in the same ditch and Overmile said, "Tell me, Sarge, do I draw double pay now?"

"Unless we hit Royce fast enough," St. Clair said, "neither of us will draw *any* pay."

"A bitter thought," Overmile said. "I'd

like one drink before I pass on."

"Water or whiskey?"

"Agh! What Irishman will drink water?" He fumbled in his shirt pocket and withdrew a sack of makings. "I dried this out some. Ain't first class, but it tastes good when there's nothin' else."

"Overmile," St. Clair said, "you're a jewel." He took the tobacco and papers and rolled himself a fat cigarette. Jim Overmile offered him a match and St. Clair bent low in the hole to screen the sudden flare. Then he sat erect and drew deeply, sighing as the sharp pinch of the tobacco hit him.

Both men sat quietly, pulling on their smokes until they were too short to handle. Overmile said, "You're sure that Royce will try to get through again?"

"Why not?" St. Clair said. "If he doesn't get ahead of us, he'll never escape with a whole hide and he knows it. Royce can't let us reach Kansas City and a telegraph station. If that happens, he'll be trapped on the river, or forced to abandon the packet. No, he'll have to make his stand here and he'll do it tonight."

"I've seen my share of rough duty," Overmile said quietly, "but I'm tellin' you now, this is the roughest I've seen it. It's possible that the lieutenant's got some explainin' to do if we get to Fort Riley. I feel for him."

St. Clair sighed heavily. "That's the price of command, Jim. An officer makes a decision and stands on it. If he's right, some colonel writes him up in a dispatch. But if the decision is wrong, the same colonel will testify at his court-martial."

"There's no real justice left in the world," Overmile said gloomily. "Here we are in the middle of nowhere, fightin' a damned war just as big as you please. Brings to mind the time I was with Scott in —" He broke off and sat upright. "What was that?"

"Be quiet," St. Clair said, and turned to face downstream. He heard the sound distinctly then, the unmistakable thump of the packet's drive rods. "In the water," he said, his voice a hoarse whisper. "On the double, men, and keep those pistols dry."

He left the trench and entered the water, Overmile right behind him. St. Clair's men edged silently into the channel, crouching until only their heads and weapons were above water.

Clouds veiled the moon and the night was mud. St. Clair strained to see the packet against the darkness of the river bank, but only the sound came to him.

They waited patiently, shivering in the river's cold, hearing the pound like a measured drum beat in the distance, drawing slowly nearer. The uneven lurch of the paddlewheel sent a pulse beat through the water and then they could see the dark bulk of the packet, heading for the narrow channel near the island.

He's smart, St. Clair thought as he watched the way Royce angled the vessel into the channel, presenting his flank and the bulk of his fire power toward the island. *Once well in he'll spin the helm hard right, add full steam and make a run for it.*

Royce made his turn and the drivers increased in tempo. Then suddenly Buckley's men opened an attack at the ridiculous range of two hundred yards. Royce steamed into the teeth of this fire for a moment, then made his decision and spun the helm again, edging close to the low island.

Buckley continued to fire by volley. From St. Clair's position in the water, the packet began to loom larger and the sound of the steam engine grew deafening. A few bullets from shore splattered the water ahead, then skipped and snapped off into the trees across the river.

Corporal Overmile and his men waited in a string and then the packet blotted them from sight. As it steamed between the two boarding parties, hands groped for the low railing.

Someone yelled in the darkness, a blend of fright and surprise, and then a pistol popped. St. Clair, pulling himself up, realized that Overmile and his men were aboard.

He dropped to the deck, and to his left and right, others bellied down. A man on the Texas turned his carbine on them and opened up. Buckley's men were raking the wheelhouse, luckily holding their fire away from the well deck where Overmile and St. Clair were rallying their men for a dash forward.

The night blossomed with muzzle flashes and Royce's men were caught between two determined foes. St. Clair made the companionway, his men close behind him. Soldiers on the upper Texas whirled to fire at them. St. Clair shot a man who leveled his carbine at him. Then he had reached the deck and began lashing out with the heavy barrel of his gun.

Overmile and the others swarmed around him in the black confusion, their pistols spouting bright flame. St. Clair and four other men made a dash to the right and managed to skirt the edge of the Texas. Buckley, seeing the criss-crossed gun flashes on the boat, understood somehow that his own men had gotten aboard and gave the order to cease fire.

Up forward, Royce was in a panic. His men were dying. Some were leaping over the side rather than face the deadly pistols in the hands of Overmile's men. The big Irishman stood on the Texas and fanned his pistol empty into Royce's scattered ranks.

"Abandon it!" Royce screamed from the other side of the wheelhouse. "Get off — get off!"

St. Clair hit the wheelhouse door and heard the lock splinter. Three men entered with him and Royce turned to fling a blind shot. One man staggered and fell against the helm, then caught himself and shot back. But Royce was gone, running aft.

Two of the troopers with St. Clair ducked into the companionway that led down into the engine room. A soldier below shot upward with his carbine and missed. The lead trooper returned the shot and did not miss.

"Stop engines!" St. Clair shouted in the voice tube and twisted the helm hard left to keep from going aground. In the engine room, guns exploded and a man cried out. Then the thumping pound of the drive rods changed cadence and stopped altogether.

The battle slacked off on the Texas deck with only spasmodic shooting aimed at the swimmers trying to make the island, now a little to the stern. Overmile's cursing was loud with frustration; he wanted Royce like a man obsessed, but Royce and the survivors of his band were getting away.

Since St. Clair's complete knowledge of seamanship had been amassed in the stern of a canoe on Skaneateles Lake one summer, he was having considerable difficulty trying to control the packet. Finally Trooper Cassidy, seeing his plight, came forward to offer his services with the announcement that he had worked on the Mississippi. St. Clair was happy to turn the helm over to more efficient hands.

Some semblance of order returned to the engine room and a moment later the drivers shook the ship. The current was swinging them about and Cassidy spun the helm hard over to assist the swing. When the bow came around, he spun the wheel in the other direction and the packet stopped, held against the current by the slowly turning wheel.

Overmile entered the wheelhouse and St. Clair asked, "What casualties do we have?"

"McDermott's gone, Sarge. Ables, McKimmie, and Carson too. Ashland has one through the thigh. The others are all right."

Cassidy called down the companionway to the engine room, "Half ahead, there!"

"Aye, aye, Admiral," came the answer. The pound of the drivers stopped, then began again. Immediately the packet gained headway and Cassidy guided it carefully through the channel past Lieutenant Buckley's position.

"Over the side," St. Clair ordered brisquely. "Report to Lieutenant Buckley that we're going out where the river is wider to turn around and beach on the island."

"I'm needin' a wettin' again," Overmile said, and a second later he splashed over the side and pushed toward shore.

Cassidy navigated the channel and when he was clear, gave the helm hard left, then called for 'stop engines.' The packet was caught half around by the current and St. Clair could feel the sideward thrust. When the current began to carry them backward and clear of the shore, Cassidy called for full speed and felt the immediate response to the helm.

When they straightened away and headed toward the island, Cassidy shouted down for slow speed and a moment later they were barely creeping against the current, until the packet ran aground smoothly. In the sudden silence, the two men could be heard talking in the engine room below, while on the Texas the other troopers called out to buddies on the shore.

Lieutenant Buckley waded out immediately and came forward. Observing the stiffness of the officer's stride across the deck, St. Clair knew that he was seething.

Buckley dismissed Cassidy from the wheelhouse, then closed the bullet-riddled door. "Sergeant St. Clair," he began, rocking back and forth on his heels, his fists clenched behind his back, "be so kind as to explain this action to me."

"I decided to board the packet, sir," St. Clair said.

"*You* decided?" Buckley's voice was deceptively mild. "St. Clair, perhaps I'm assuming too much when I fancy myself in command of this expedition." He waved his hand. "Perhaps the strain has been too great for me and I'm harboring delusions that I gave you an order that did not embrace a marine assault. *Will you straighten me out on this, Sergeant?*"

St. Clair took an involuntary backward step at the explosive tone. A wave of self righteousness swept his training aside and his anger flared. "Leave it to you, sir, and we'd be here until doomsday!"

"I see," Buckley said. "Perhaps you considered my orders overcautious?"

"Yes, sir. I did."

"And perhaps I'm a martinet, a stickler for details. Is that it?"

"Yes, sir," St. Clair said.

"May I inform you, Sergeant, that the glory road is blocked by corpses. Men who dreamed that combat was filled with dash and splendor. For your information, St. Clair, the Army is composed of routine, one stinking, piddling routine piled upon another. I trust this information is penetrating your skull?"

"Yes, sir," St. Clair said in a low voice, standing at attention. He was still angry but something compelling in Lieutenant Buckley's manner drew his respect. "May — may I speak, sir?"

"Do you think you have anything important to say?"

"No, sir," St. Clair admitted.

Buckley sighed and removed his sweat-stained hat, mopping hair away from his forehead. "I offer my congratulations for your success. It will go in your dossier — along with my reprimand."

"Thank you, sir."

"For what? The commendation or the reprimand?" He smiled faintly. "You still don't see why you deserve a reprimand, do you?"

"No, sir."

"Some day," Buckley said, "you may learn a few facts about soldiering, St. Clair. One of them is that there can be only *one* commanding officer, and right or wrong, you owe him your loyalty. You have dash and guts enough to carry you through, but given a choice, I'd not have you in my command. I doubt that any able officer would disagree with me."

He turned on his heel and went out, barking orders, organizing his troop for boarding.

St. Clair stood there numbly. *I'd not have you in my command! I'd not have you in my command! I'd not have you . . .*

The words were branded on his brain.

CHAPTER 11

Lieutenant Buckley was appalled by the fact that he could load the remaining men aboard the one packet. He recalled only too vividly how crowded *four* packets had been at the outset of this journey.

Lieutenant McAuliff was in sore need of skilled attention. He was delirious intermittently and Buckley was soberly conscious of the chance of gangrene in the man's arm. They tried to move McAuliff into the captain's quarters, but momentarily lucid, he protested and would not quiet down until the room was promised to Peg Delaney.

During the remaining hours of the night, the wounded were moved aboard and made as comfortable as possible. Buckley posted guards although he had little fear that Royce would return with fewer than a half-dozen followers left in his force.

St. Clair found an isolated spot abaft the wheelhouse and stretched out to sleep. The strong light of the sun woke him and he sat up, pawing at his eyes.

The cloud layer had broken and a new warmth flowed over the land. St. Clair came off the wheelhouse roof and found Sergeant Delaney and Buckley making ready to get under way.

Buckley, his face dark with beard, stood at the wheelhouse door and spoke to the trooper inside. "In view of your handling last night, Cassidy, I think you must be the master seaman in this troop. Steam ahead half speed and watch out for sunken logs. I'm not interested in haste, Trooper — just safety. Get us up-river."

"I'll do my best, sir," Cassidy said, and called down to the engine room for power. He backed off the island, and once clear, called for half ahead and steered the packet through the channel. St. Clair joined Cassidy in the wheelhouse and at noon, Peg Delaney came in with a pint of scalding coffee for them.

Her face was clean now and her hair had been washed and braided high on her head. St. Clair took the coffee and asked, "How did you manage that?" He nodded toward her glistening hair.

"Trooper Matthews drew me a bucket of water from the boilers. It was a little rusty, but nice and hot."

He smiled. "I appoint you a detail of one

to find me a razor, seeing as how you are so original."

Her face went suddenly white and she looked at him with stricken eyes. "Quincy, don't talk about razors now." She shuddered. "Buckley says Lieutenant McAuliff's arm has to come off."

She turned as boots rattled along the Texas and then Buckley paused in the wheelhouse door. "Cassidy, pull this scow onto the first wooded beach you come to. We need firewood and there's a job to be done that needs steadiness. We'll do it better if we're not in motion."

"Yes, sir," Cassidy said, and studied the banks. He steamed on for better than three quarters of an hour, then rounded a long bend and spied a beach to the right. Calling for half power, he edged the packet close to shore, then ordered the engine stopped and drifted in.

Immediately, a wood-cutting detail left the boat, and soon the ring of an axe smote their ears. Peg Delaney took a cigar from the pocket of the trooper's shirt she wore. "Here," she said in a strained voice. "I've swore off."

St. Clair took the smoke with a murmured thanks and sniffed it with his eyes closed. He licked it carefully, then snipped off the end with his teeth. On shore, the sudden crash of falling timber muffled the strident noise of the axe. He put a match to the cigar and leaned against the door frame.

In the well deck below, men's voices made an indistinct rumble, and then a rich tenor began to sing:

. . . "Oh, she jumped in bed and covered up her head . . ."

"They've got McAuliff drunk," Peg said and bit her lip.

St. Clair stepped from the doorway as though to leave, but Peg blocked him. "Don't go! Stay here with me."

". . . But I knew damn well she lied like hell so I jumped . . ."

A deeper voice floated up. "Easy now, sor. Get that bucket of flour ready, O'Toole."

". . . My gal Sal is a dirty little gal, and she's always rea . . . Aaaagggggghhhhhh!"

The sound was a burst and festered sore and the echo of it hung obscene over the river. Peg Delaney clapped her hands over her ears and pushed her forehead against the bulkhead, crying uncontrollably. St. Clair's teeth vised on the cigar and severed it. He spat out the soggy end and held his expression rigid.

"Oooooohhhhhhh!" McAuliff's voice was no longer human.

There was the sound of thrashing as eight strong men held him down for the saw. His screaming went off the scale and it seemed to fill the land until a man could never go far enough away to escape the awful vibration of it.

The ring of the axe broke again upon their consciousness, and on the well deck troopers swore in dull, flat tones.

Then McAuliff fell silent and the absence of the scream was like the shock of a thunderclap. Peg Delaney pulled her face away from the wall. She turned slowly to look at Quincy St. Clair who stood absolutely motionless, his complexion gray.

Someone threw a cloth bound bundle over the side, the splash too loud in the silence. St. Clair rekindled his dead cigar with shaking hands, while Peg rubbed her face aimlessly with the back of her hand.

Lieutenant Buckley came up to the Texas deck and paused by the wheelhouse, his expression haggard. His voice was even quieter than usual. "As soon as the woodcutting detail returns, have Cassidy back off and proceed upstream."

"Yes, sir," St. Clair said. "Mr. McAuliff — how is he?"

"Bad off," Buckley said bluntly. "We have a five day run facing us. We'll try to keep him alive for the contract surgeon. That's all we can do."

The wood detail came aboard an hour later and stowed the fuel near the boilers. McAuliff was moved to the mate's cabin, a five-by-seven cubicle that bunked three. Peg Delaney insisted on vacating the captain's quarters, a room no larger than the mate's, for the more seriously wounded troopers. Thereafter she slept in the small wheelhouse on the chart table.

Cassidy warped the packet into the dock with a minimum of effort, butted against the piling with a slight jar, and the bow and stern lines were made fast.

An Army ambulance waited on the dock, along with a mudwagon and ten mounted troopers. First to leave the packet, Lieutenant Buckley went forward to meet the group of officers standing on the dock. From the Texas, St. Clair studied this group of men.

Buckley saluted and made his report, drawing deep frowns from the major and captain. The three lieutenants stood unconcerned.

Major Justin Baker shook hands with

Buckley and introduced the officers, with the exception of Captain Ackerman, a tall blond man with a clipped beard.

"Lieutenant Woodmyer, Lieutenant Pindelist, Lieutenant Gordon. Lieutenant Buckley, gentlemen." He cleared his throat. "Get your troopers off the packet, Buckley. Mr. Gordon, see to a temporary bivouac for these men."

"Yes, sir," Gordon said, saluting. He wheeled away and began to snap orders at the sergeant and ten troopers.

"Lieutenant Buckley, my temporary command post is that lumber office over there." He pointed to a small shed at the end of the dirt street. "Assemble your officers and meet me there in ten minutes. I want a detailed report of this action."

Major Baker rotated on his heel and stalked away, his retinue following. Buckley returned to the packet, placed Corporal Overmile in charge of unloading, and took Sergeant St. Clair and Sergeant Delaney with him.

Walking the length of the dock, Buckley explained this meeting. "Both of you are soldiers enough to know the spot I'm in. Answer their questions clearly and honestly. The responsibility is mine, no matter how this comes out."

The three lieutenants were absent when Buckley entered the building with his two sergeants. Major Baker sat behind a scarred desk, cigar smoke wreathing his head and shoulders. Captain Ackerman turned away from the window.

"I left you with two able officers," he said. "Buckley, I demand an accounting of this sordid affair!"

"We'll get it," Baker said, shooting Ackerman a glance that warned him to keep his proper respect for rank. He looked at Sergeant Delaney, then at St. Clair. "I don't believe I recognize you, Sergeant. Are you new to the regiment?"

"Yes, sir," St. Clair said. "First enlistment, sir."

"Hmmm," Baker said, stroking his mustache. "Rapid promotion."

"I request permission to question Lieutenant Buckley," Captain Ackerman said.

"Permission granted," Baker said, leaning back in his chair.

"Will you please explain to me," Ackerman asked, "how you could lose sixty percent of your command to one rebellious troop whose strength was little more than a platoon?"

"They were supported by several hundred Sioux Indians," Buckley said. "Major, my men can uphold that statement."

Baker's eyes flicked to St. Clair. "How many hostiles would you say were in the first attacking force?"

"No less than two hundred, sir. The plan was clever and well executed. With Sergeant Royce's sudden withdrawal at the most crucial moment, and his subsequent attack, the main force aboard the other three packets was hopelessly outnumbered."

"I didn't ask for a lesson in tactics," Captain Ackerman said tartly. He paced back and forth in the small room, shooting Buckley hostile glances. "Lieutenant, your sole purpose was to march to this station, gather reenforcements, then proceed to a field assignment. Instead, you allow yourself to be tricked by an enlisted man, engage in a prolonged and costly fight, and in the end stand before me with the impertinent story that you were detained by a force of platoon strength. Lieutenant, do you think me a fool?"

"No, sir," Buckley said. "But under the circumstances, I challenge the captain to have handled himself with more effect, sir."

Captain Ackerman looked like a man about to have a stroke. His color deepened and his clipped beard fairly bristled. Major

Baker coughed gently and waved his hand.

"Gentlemen," he said. "I think this discussion is on the verge of getting out of hand. Lieutenant Buckley, during the march to the Smoky Hill, I want a detailed written report embracing this action, with the causes and effects. I am more concerned now with the task of bringing the Second to the strength needed to accomplish our mission. A runner will be sent to Fort Leavenworth, ordering Captain Marquis to reassign three troops. We'll rendezvous at Fort Riley in a week. That's all, gentlemen."

He answered their salutes and they filed out, Captain Ackerman closing the door. He spoke to Buckley. "I'm not pleased at all, Jules."

"No less than I am," Buckley said evenly. "I lost good men on this march, sir."

"And I'm not satisfied it wasn't in vain," Ackerman said.

"I'm prepared to accept full responsibility," Buckley assured him.

"That is one thing of which I am certain," Ackerman said and walked away, his hard hitting heels raising small echoes on the planks.

The three men watched him until he disappeared up the street. Then Sergeant

Delaney said, "Beggin' the Lieutenant's pardon, sor, but he don't seem too happy that we made it."

"Button your lip," Buckley said, his voice low and undisturbed.

Major Baker came from the shack, drawing on his gauntlets. He stepped up to Buckley and said, "Privately, Lieutenant, I think your conduct was commendable, but Captain Ackerman is your commanding officer. If he prefers charges of dereliction of duty, I can only process them."

"I quite understand, sir," Buckley said. "Has the captain been this — agitated for long?"

Baker gnawed on his lower lip. "Yes, he has. You were due in three days ago, and he has been pacing the dock like an expectant father." He brightened then and offered Buckley a cigar and a light. Major Baker was a soldier with twenty-seven years of Army under his belt, and from long habit he ignored Sergeant Delaney and St. Clair. He spoke to Buckley as if they were alone.

"There isn't much of a cantonment at Ellsworth," he said. "A small palisade and a bivouac area. We can billet the officers and families all right — oh, I'm sorry. I forgot that you'd already been there."

"Will we have sufficient officers?" Buckley asked.

"There are several on their way from Eastern assignments," Baker said. "One is fresh from the Plain. I expect the usual run of trouble for the first six months until they get acquainted with frontier procedure." He curled a forefinger around his cigar and drew on it. "The command will be broken up into detachments to follow the wire camps as they move forward. Western Union headquarters at Omaha hasn't yet decided whether the line is going south along the Santa Fe to Bent's Fort or across the Rockies farther north. A great deal depends on the Indian troubles. There's a line camp south of Hays City, if you can call a road ranch and a saloon a town. They've suffered three raids in the last month. I imagine a troop will be sent in there to clean that out."

"Have you any idea who's behind the Indian trouble, sir?"

Baker looked sharply at the lieutenant. "I think I know what's behind it, Buckley. In Captain Ackerman's report, he denies that there's a Southern movement designed to cripple the telegraph line." He took his cigar from his mouth and stepped on it. "Get some rest, Buckley. I've detailed the contract surgeon to care for your wounded. But for the sake of appearance, I would muster to duty as many men as you can before the replacements arrive. Makes it look better that way."

Sergeants Delaney and St. Clair came to attention with clicking heels and Lieutenant Buckley answered Major Baker's salute before he walked away.

"If you'll excuse me, sor, I'll get on with me duties," Sergeant Delaney said and walked the length of the dock to help the last of the troop vacate the packet. The wounded were being carried off while the able-bodied formed ranks and took care of what equipment remained.

Buckley stood with feet apart and stroked his mustache with his forefinger. "You passed up a golden opportunity to nail me to the wall in there. I wouldn't have blamed you if you had. Neither will I thank you for not expressing your opinion. For a moment I thought you had learned something, but I can see that it was the gentleman cropping out. When we reach our station, I want you to keep a sharp eye on Captain Ackerman."

"I intend to do that, sir," St. Clair said.

CHAPTER 12

A week of rest and proper discipline did much to restore the morale of the men. With Lieutenant Buckley in command — Captain Ackerman absented himself considerably — the three remaining troops were soon whipped into shape. Buckley's code, although meticulously exact in every detail, was also scrupulously fair. He seemed to possess an almost uncanny understanding of a trooper's mind.

St. Clair found himself occupied with routine duties during the week and found no opportunity to visit Peg Delaney, who was staying in town at a private home. Toward the end of the week eighty mounted men rode onto the crowded parade and dismounted.

Captain Ackerman made an appearance then and announced that the entire command would take to the field with march equipment an hour after mess call in the morning.

The rest of the day was spent in readying mounts and men. Ackerman was a difficult officer to please, St. Clair discovered. The man seemed to take delight in picking up a small irregularity and building it into a large production. Buckley, however, appeared undisturbed by Ackerman's interference and went on getting the job done.

All this St. Clair observed with a certain abstract interest, for the machinations of command on the enlisted level bored him. Only the actual movement of troops in the field appealed to him, for therein lay the true blaze and dash of cavalry duty. For a time he had felt this on the river where the essence of command had been in his hands. The fighting had taken on flavor — the charge, the swift counter movements that were the core of the cavalry, the sole excuse for its existence, had become a personal challenge that he had met successfully. Even though Lieutenant Buckley had disapproved his actions. . . .

He remembered Peg Delaney's words, her observation that he could never be content as an enlisted man. She was right, he admitted. He was an officer by training, by instinct. Command was his function. Not the staid, middle-of-the-road command of Buckley, but the daring do-or-die tactics that had marked Hannibal and Genghis Khan.

The next morning the troops were formed, and marched across the parade with Captain Ackerman at the head. Lieutenant Buckley commanded the escort wagons, a job he detested.

Cavalry on the march was monotonous. Continual dust, the noise, the odor of horses and men — these things worked on troopers' nerves until each night when bivouac was reached, silence hung like a curtain over the encampment until hot coffee softened the day's tedium. Each night Captain Ackerman's tent was erected, and troopers had to carry and heat water for his bath. On the third evening he held a full field inspection and nearly incited a mutiny. A soldier is not in the mood to polish his gear after a fifty-five mile forced march.

Buckley stayed with the escort wagons. The three new officers formed a mutual admiration society, excluding all others. Uncertain of themselves, they felt every trooper their enemy, ready to have a laugh at their expense. Captain Ackerman did nothing to relieve this situation and the march was a sullen one at best.

The cantonment, south of the new town of Ellsworth, brought sharp disappointment, for the palisade was small, rough,

219

and scarcely half finished. With no permanent stables, horses had to be kept on the picket rope, thereby doubling the troopers' guard duties.

Contrary to his orders to move into the field, Captain Ackerman insisted that the command finish the post — a job already pre-assigned to an Engineer battalion due to arrive later in the year. For weeks the area around the fort rang with the strokes of axes and new walls went up rapidly. New buildings took shape and troopers grew more discontented.

At the end of the first week, St. Clair and his men were pulled off the construction details and he found Overmile waiting at the end of the new barracks. The sun slanted its last rays across the land and the fresh peeled logs were honey-colored.

"You missed it, Sarge," Overmile said. "The new officers arrived on the paymaster's coach this afternoon." He jerked his thumb toward the orderly room across the parade. "The lieutenant wants to see you."

"Thanks," St. Clair said. He trotted across the parade. He entered Buckley's office and the clerk closed the door.

"Pull up a chair," Buckley said, and offered St. Clair a cigar. "Got word from town this afternoon, and there's some moguls from Western Union who want to see you. Delaney will make arrangements for transportation. This has to look natural."

"Thanks for the cigar, sir," St. Clair said, and returned to his barracks. He met Sergeant Delaney coming from the new stable and stopped. Darkness was descending rapidly, one of those black prairie nights where even the vastness is swallowed up.

Delaney said, "Promoted an ambulance for you. Peg's goin' in and that's your ride."

"When are you leaving?"

"Thirty minutes."

"I'll be ready." St. Clair went on to the barracks to brush his uniform. He changed his shirt and shaved. The sergeant chevrons felt stiff against his arms. He donned his yellow lined coat, frogged it, and gave the visor of his kepi a final tug. He had made it a rule never to leave the post without his .44 Dragoon, and the coat made an excellent cover for the shoulder holster, yet gave him ready access in case of need.

He adjusted the strap of his forager cap, then sauntered out into the darkness. There was something about a cavalry post at night that he liked. The dark parade ground, lined on one side by the sprinkling

221

of lamplight shining in the officers' picket quarters, the soft movement of guards as they wove along the perimeter of the palisade — all this lent a sense of peace absent in the daytime.

Skirting the edge of the married officers' row, he halted when a door was suddenly flung wide, spilling out a shaft of light that struck him boldly. The slender outline of a young woman was silhouetted for a moment, then the door shut with a slam and blackness again enveloped him. Puzzled, he hesitated a moment longer, then decided it was no concern of his and hurried on to headquarters.

From the high, front seat of the ambulance, Peg Delaney said, "Come on, Pokey. I'll be late for my dinner."

"Where's your father?"

"He can't come," Peg said. "Important business."

"This sounds contrived," he teased, and mounted the seat beside her.

She laughed at him. "Truthfully, it was, but he didn't mind staying on the post. You've neglected me, Quincy, and I'm not sure I ought to let you get away with it."

"We'll argue about it on the way," he said, and kicked off the brake, driving toward the main gate. The sentry came close to the off wheel after halting them, then passed them and they rolled free of the post.

Peg settled back on the hard seat. As wagons went, the army ambulance had enough springs but the high square box made the rig topheavy. If a man wasn't used to it, he could get seasick going over a rough road.

The team moved along at a fair clip and twenty minutes brought them to Ellsworth, a sprawling town with a new wildness of its own. St. Clair decided that this town had a far different feel from Crystal City. Here each man wore a gun and a knife; some wore two pistols. This was the West and whatever law there was rested in each man's ability to enforce it.

Ellsworth lay on the flat bank of the Smoky Hill River, a drab, ulcerous growth on the bosom of the land. The treeless plaza, fetlock deep in dust, separated the scant dozen buildings. St. Clair looked at it wonderingly and said, "What holds it together? Where's the business come from?"

"People passing through," Peg said. "See that mound of dirt running the length of the street?" She pointed. "There's a railroad going in there some day; that's what a handful of people who built this town believe. There's the ticket office over there."

On the far side of the plaza, the ticket office reared up alone and unpainted. St. Clair stared at it, then drove on down the street and tied the team at the hitch-rail.

To all appearances this building served as a hotel; the bottom floor was devoted to the service of drinkers and a lot of noise blared forth. St. Clair helped Peg dismount and they went up the stairs together, using a side entrance reserved for pimps and young boys carrying buckets of beer to the guests.

Once on the upper floor, they traveled the length of a hall and she rapped on a door. Wade Garland opened it, smiling as he saw St. Clair. "Come in," he said, and closed the door behind them. He took Peg's cape and waited for St. Clair's. The young man removed it reluctantly and Wade Garland looked amused when he saw the heavy Colt pistol. "Going bear hunting?" he asked.

"Skunk," St. Clair amended, and settled in a soft chair. Alex Howison came from the bedroom and St. Clair rose to shake hands.

"Congratulations," Howison said. "You turned a neat trick in Crystal City."

Peg Delaney turned and looked at

Howison. St. Clair said, "News travels fast."

"Yes," Howison said. He studied the tip of his cigar. "Buckley sent a report. I thought you knew."

"No, I didn't know. You hear about the fight we had on the river?"

"Splendid job there," Howison agreed. "The talk's all over town. I'm afraid you're becoming rather well known."

"I'd sooner remain anonymous. Royce is still at large and that bothers me. Does it bother you?"

"Some," Howison admitted. "Wade, when are they going to bring up that meal?"

"I'll go see," Garland said. He left the room.

Howison sat down and crossed his legs. "I intend to move Buckley into the field; he can do his best work there. We'll not be alarmed about Royce now. Being on the dodge, there's little he could do now to hinder a westward push with wire."

"Something's been bothering me," St. Clair said bluntly. "I wonder how Royce found out about me so quickly. That night I went into Crystal City, I wasn't supposed to come back. Ask Peg, she can tell you."

"That *was* a deliberate try for his life,

Mr. Howison," Peg said, "and both my father and Jules feel the same way."

"They're slick," Howison said, slapping the arm of his chair. "You'll have to be careful, lad. Mighty careful." The door opened and Garland ushered in a man with a large tray. "We'll talk after we eat," Howison said, and cleared a table.

There had been nothing to prepare Glorianna Upton for the raw shock of seeing Sergeant St. Clair standing in the light from her door. She had stiffened involuntarily, mortally afraid that he would speak, and then unaccountably hurt when he did not.

Slamming the door, she leaned back against it.

Niles Upton raised his head. He had been arranging his uniforms on the wall rack. "Do you have to bang things like that?"

"Sorry." She moved away from the door. Her trunk was standing in the middle of the drab room, still unpacked. She lacked the will to open it.

Throwing down a suit of soiled blues, Upton snapped, "Is that all you can say — 'sorry'? You've been saying it now for ten beastly days and I'm sick of hearing it!"

"You don't have to shout."

"Shout! I feel like screaming." He waved a hand at the fresh peeled logs. "How primitive does an officer have to get? By God, at least they could furnish decent quarters!"

"I'm surprised you're not blaming me for it," Glorianna said wearily. "Aren't you ever going to forgive me, Niles?"

"The very thought is obscene," he said. "Please, let me finish my unpacking. You have your own trunk to do. Why don't you get at it?"

"Later," she said. "I think I'll go out for a bit of air."

He didn't reply and she opened the door and stepped out into the darkness, grateful for the privacy night afforded. She walked slowly toward regimental headquarters, a low building with lamplight shining from the windows. Ahead of her a sergeant stepped out and she said, "Pardon me. I'm Lieutenant Upton's wife. Perhaps you could tell me something."

"Yes, ma'am," Sergeant Delaney said, removing his kepi. "What is it, ma'am?"

"I — there was a soldier, a sergeant, who passed by here a few minutes ago. He was heading this way. I wonder if you could tell me his name."

"Let's see," Delaney said, frowning. "No one's come into headquarters, ma'am. Oh, you must mean Sergeant St. Clair, ma'am. He took the ambulance to town."

"St. Clair? That name means nothing to me. Sorry to have troubled you, Sergeant."

"Not at all, ma'am," Delaney said, and pulled at his lower lip as she moved away. He began to add it up in his mind, merely to see what kind of answer he would get. He had seen Lieutenant Upton's orders: graduating class of 1857. Simply put, Upton must be known to St. Clair. Friends? Delaney wondered about it.

He walked on to his barracks, his head down, pondering this.

Returning to her quarters, Glorianna wondered what she should do. Tell Niles that Quincy St. Clair was here? If she withheld the information, she would probably be accused of hiding something. She decided it would be best to come out with it.

She found him in a hard-backed chair, boning his parade boots. Closing the door, she put her shoulders against it and said, "Niles, Quincy St. Clair is on the post."

She had taken pains to speak mildly, with a certain amount of disinterest, but he reacted like a man shot. Leaping from the chair, he dashed to his locker, took out his pistol and tried to force her away from the door.

"Have you gone insane?" She yelled this at him.

He struck at her but she kept her place, blocking his way. "Niles, for heaven's sake, stop making such a fuss! Do you want the other officers to hear us fighting?"

This calmed him as nothing else could have. He stood there, breathing heavily, his Colt pistol dangling at arm's length. "You knew he was here!" he accused.

"How could I have known? What possible difference would it have made anyway? I never loved him."

This wrung a wry laugh from him. "You never loved him. How like you, Glorianna." He smiled without humor. "I'll see him dead. I'll want you to know when he's dead and then I'll laugh when the baby is born. I'll be able to look at it and know that I killed its father."

She put her hands to her face. "You're absolutely out of your mind! Crazy!"

"I expected you to deny it," he said. "It doesn't matter. I have patience and I'll get him. I'll do it cleverly enough so that no one will ever know. But in the end I'll have my revenge."

She was quiet for a long moment, and

then she said, "Niles, if I had this to do over again, I don't think I'd want you for a husband under any circumstances."

He hit her blindly with his fist, rapping her head against the door. She sank to the floor, her legs suddenly too weak to hold her. She let her head tip forward and blood from her nose made small red spots on the bare floor.

But she didn't cry.

CHAPTER 13

Wade Garland set out brandy and cigars, then watered a drink for Peg Delaney before settling himself in an easy chair. He raised his drink in salute. "To the most resourceful young man I know, even though he's often in hot water."

They drank while St. Clair found a moment of confusion.

"I think," Garland went on, "we can consider this adventure a success so far." He tabulated it on his fingers. "First, Rance Ranier has always been a thorn where it hurts. Lieutenant Michaels, the first officer we had, ran afoul of Ranier and was killed. To all appearances it was above board, but he was no less dead and we had to start all over again. Looking back on it, I can see where Michaels didn't have a chance.

"Captain Osterman, our second choice, was accosted by Ranier but proved a little smarter and got as far as Fort Riley. He was killed there while on patrol, in a brush with jayhawkers. Sergeant Royce was along

231

on that patrol, and now I wonder if he didn't shoot the captain himself.

"But you seem to eliminate the opposition as you go along. Ranier is gone. Royce, long suspected as an active hireling for the Southern cause, has been reduced to ineffectiveness. Young man, your record to date is remarkable."

"I'm afraid I deserve little credit," St. Clair said uncomfortably. "The shooting of Ranier was thrust upon me and the routing of Royce was more accident than design."

Garland pushed this aside with a wave of his hand. "I don't care whether a man is shaved by a barber or uses his Bowie knife as long as he presents a clean face. Don't you agree, Alex?"

"Yes," Howison said. He laid his cigar aside and replenished his brandy. "St. Clair, there's a copperhead behind every bush here. The people resent the cavalry but there have been no open flareups as yet. Missouri, of course, is Southern, but Kansas intends to remain neutral. That term can be misleading, however, for there are many here who work for the South. They don't go around shouting this and they often strike without warning."

"What Howison is saying," Garland said, "is that many officers in the military are from the South and thereby Southern in sympathy. There are only a handful to turn to and you already know them, so trust no one. We have, to all appearances, an Indian problem on our hands. Somehow they've managed to get muskets and powder and the unrest is growing against the 'singing wire.' It's my personal belief that this concentration of Southern effort is intended to hamstring the telegraph in this area. Now we have troops and we have you. I want to see something done about it."

"We're assigning a scout to Lieutenant Buckley," Howison said. "His name is Hardin and he's good, as skilled as you'll find. In a day or two, you'll take to the field and check our forward pole camp. We're using it now as a communications link with the surveyors in the field. Keep your eyes open, St. Clair. In all probability you're a marked man."

"Not a cheerful thought," St. Clair admitted. "Frankly, I'm a bit discouraged. It does little good to eliminate men like Royce and Ranier when we still have no idea who the top man is."

"That will come in time," Garland assured him. "It's enough for now that you've gone a long way toward cutting the legs out from under the 'top man.' Without them, he'll surely be hampered in his operations."

"I hope so, sir," St. Clair said. He gathered his coat and kepi, helped Peg into her cape, then shook hands with Garland and Howison.

"We're going to remain on the frontier a while," Howison said. "The hostility we encounter here will of course determine our final decision as to whether the wire will go west from Omaha, or slant south to Bent's Fort. It will have to be decided soon. The cost in time is already considerable."

They parted at the door and St. Clair escorted Peg down the side stairs to the ambulance. There was now little traffic on the street and he made a U turn, driving immediately from town. Once the buildings were behind them, he held the team to a walk.

Peg said, "I don't think I like your job."

"It has disadvantages," he admitted. "Keeps me away from home nights. But then I have no home, so how important is that?" On impulse, he braked the ambulance to the side of the narrow road and wrapped the reins around the brake handle. "Peg," he said, "have you ever been anything but completely honest?"

"I've tried not to be," she said softly.

"I can't make up my mind whether you'd be a wonderful wife or simply hell to live with. If your husband came home from a four-day patrol, dirty, in need of a shave, you'd open the door — being completely honest — and say, 'You look simply —.' "

" 'Gorgeous,' I'd say, and 'I love you very much!' " She had meant to keep her answer in the same light vein established by him, but her feelings became involved and the statement tripped her, revealing something she had wished to keep hidden.

He touched her arm, slid his hand to her shoulder, and waited. "Peg, once we kissed because we needed each other. Now the circumstances are a little different. You no longer need me, but I find I still need you."

Putting his hand on her back, he pulled her to him. He was gentle with her because his emotion was gentle. One of her arms encircled him. The other crept around his neck, and their kiss was what they both wanted, containing the essence of tomorrow's dreams, the feeling that lovers have of belonging for eternities.

When their lips parted, they sat silently for a time. Finally St. Clair said, "Peg, I love you. I want to marry you."

She touched his face. Then she remembered another man's words and her hand flattened against his chest, pushing until she sat apart from him on her side of the seat. "I'm sorry, Quincy. I shouldn't have allowed you to do this to me."

"Peg, what is it? Don't push me out."

"Take me back to the post," she said. "Quincy, don't you understand? I'm not for you or any other man."

"No, I don't understand," he said, and unwrapped the reins.

The ride back was a silent one with Peg in her corner, wanting to explain the unexplainable to him, while he groped blindly for the reasons behind her behavior, his mind sparked with the thin information gleaned aboard the packet the night she was ill.

When he could tolerate this no longer, he said, "If it has anything to do with 'Jim,' then tell me and we'll get the air cleared once and for all."

"I can't tell you," she said. "He's dead, if that bothers you."

"It doesn't bother me," he told her, "but it evidently bothers you. You're acting like a child."

"All right, so I'm a child!" She was crying now. "If I'm so bothersome, let me out and I'll walk the rest of the way!"

He knew she had no intention of leaving, but she was upset and unreasonable, so he held his peace. At the palisade, the sentry opened the gates and they rolled through. St. Clair drove directly to her quarters off the end of officers' row. He left her at the door and no word was spoken. Leading the horses, he angled toward the stables with the ambulance.

Behind him, the door to Lieutenant Upton's quarters opened. Upton peered out, then ducked back inside, reappearing a moment later to pad across the dusty parade after the highsided ambulance.

In the stables, St. Clair turned the horses into separate stalls, straightened out the harness on wall pegs, then took the lantern to leave. He stopped in the archway when Lieutenant Niles Upton said, "Set down the lantern and come over here, Sergeant!"

Placing the light on the ground, St. Clair walked toward the voice. Upton was leaning against the side of the stable, his hands across his stomach.

"Surprised, Sergeant?"

"Not especially, sir. Should I be?"

"You're a cool one," Upton said softly. "I've been assigned as your platoon officer. I'll warn you now that I expect a most meticulous adherence to detail from you. One infraction and I'll have those stripes."

"A little hazing, sir?"

"I'll more than haze you, dammit! I'll run your hind end into a hole and cover it up before I'm through. I'll drive you over the hill and have you brought back just to drive you over again."

"I don't understand," St. Clair said, genuinely puzzled. "You're talking like a crazy man, Niles."

Upton's voice shook with anger. "Stand at attention when you talk to an officer! Say 'sir' when you address me, do you understand?"

"No, I don't — sir. You're coming apart, Niles."

"I'll have you in the stockade for this," Upton said, and slashed St. Clair across the face with his gauntlets. St. Clair rocked forward and Upton pulled a gun from inside his waistband. "Go ahead, raise your hand to me and I'll shoot you where you stand for threatening an officer!"

He cocked the gun, holding it against St. Clair's stomach.

Behind them, Sergeant Delaney stepped suddenly from the deep shadows. Upton wheeled, then checked himself as the faint splash of lantern light touched the grizzled sergeant. "A little trouble here, sor?"

Delaney's voice was mild. "You go on now, sor, and I'll handle this for you. An officer like yourself ought not get involved with a trooper, sor."

On the verge of refusal, Upton hesitated, then uncocked his gun and stalked across the parade. St. Clair raised his hand to his forehead and found that he was sweating.

"I didn't know you were there, Delaney."

"I was comin' from headquarters when I saw the lieutenant followin' you. So I just edged back in the dark and waited." Delaney peered after Upton's retreating figure. "The man has a great hate for you, lad. You were at the Point together?"

"Yes," St. Clair said. "We were never friends, but I can't explain this attitude."

"I saw the lieutenant's wife this evenin'," Delaney said. "She asked about you."

"Me?" He was alarmed and angered without knowing why. "Did she give you her name?"

"No, but I looked it up in the lieutenant's jacket. It was Glorianna."

St. Clair stood in shocked silence for a minute. Then he said, "I see," and walked slowly toward his barracks.

Directly after mess the next morning, Sergeant St. Clair walked across the parade and entered regimental headquarters. He was admitted immediately into Major Baker's office.

"At ease," the major said. He lifted Buckley's written report from his desk. "I'm not overly impressed with your conduct, Sergeant, but the results please me." St. Clair flushed. "I'm the top man — Captain Buckley's superior in this mission."

"Captain, sir?"

"Yes," Baker said. "His promotion came through yesterday afternoon. You'll ration and quarter with C Troop, Sergeant. Captain Buckley is taking to the field this afternoon. I want you with him. Get your cantle-roll oat issue from the quartermaster and see that the remount sergeant gives you a sound horse. Report here at noon work call with full ammunition and rations for five days."

"Very good, sir," St. Clair said. He saluted and performed a precise about-face.

"Oh, St. Clair."

"Yes, sir." Another about-face.

The major was smiling. "I haven't seen that maneuver performed with such precision since I left the Point. Hereafter, put a little sloppiness into it. Anyone with a lick of sense could see that you're more than a sergeant."

"I'll try, sir." Another salute and then he was out of the building and crossing the parade at a loose-legged walk. The post was alive with activity. Troopers wheeled their mounts in unified drill while sergeants called cadence to marching men. Along the east wall, a dismounted platoon wheeled in saber drill, the bright steel flashing in the bland sun.

At the quartermaster's shed, St. Clair made his cantle-roll, signing the chit before leaving. At the remount stables he inspected several horses, then selected a full-chested animal with no visible flaws. Reserving this horse, he returned to his barracks and made up his pack, checked his carbine and went to the ordnance sergeant for an extra ration of ammunition. He drew a canvas beltful and took this to the stable where his saddle hung on a stall.

In a nearby area, Lieutenant Upton schooled his platoon in dry firing, practice loading and squeezing without live ammunition. Turning his head to dress down some laggard, he saw Sergeant St. Clair enter the stable. Detailing the platoon to Corporal Overmile, he strode toward St. Clair, his heels striking sharp and angry.

"Sergeant!" He used his best parade ground voice.

"Yes, sir," St. Clair said, coming to attention.

"You were absent from work call this morning, Sergent. I find that intolerable."

"Official business, sir."

"There is no official business for you unless I'm informed of it," Upton snapped. "What was the nature of this pressing matter? Some low-de-dow with a woman?"

"I decline to answer, respectfully," St. Clair said. "Perhaps Captain Buckley would inform the Lieutenant. I'm unable to."

Upton's lips twitched. "Sergeant, I gave you a direct command." Upton saw that St. Clair was not going to obey and he looked around, spotting the farrier sergeant at his forge. "Sergeant! You there! Come here."

The farrier sergeant approached, saluted, and waited uncertainly.

"Sergeant, see that this man's things are returned to his barracks."

"Yes, sir," the sergeant said and half-turned away.

"Leave them," St. Clair said in a clear voice and Upton pulled his breath in sharply.

"You heard that order, Sergeant!"

"If the Lieutenant will inform himself,"

St. Clair said, "he will discover I am detached from his platoon. Orders from regiment."

"You lie," Upton accused. "You're lying to escape a detail. By God, I'll show you how I deal with a mutinous trooper." He flipped his head toward the waiting farrier sergeant. "Have you a wagon?"

"In the back, sir. Beggin' the lieutenant's pardon, sir, but I'd check first."

Upton froze the man with his eyes. "Are you telling me how to exact discipline, Sergeant?"

"Oh, no, sir!"

"March ahead of me, St. Clair," Upton ordered.

"You may regret this, sir," St. Clair said, and went around the building. The farrier sergeant shot St. Clair a sympathetic glance, but he was an old soldier and this type of punishment was not new to him. He could see that St. Clair was on the verge of rebellion and he spoke softly. "Whatever it is, take it and be done with it."

Lieutenant Upton crossed to the wall for a coiled whip and St. Clair said, "Get away and get Captain Buckley. On the double, man!"

"All right," the farrier sergeant said, and

stood aside as Upton snaked the whip out behind him.

"Strip to the waist," he ordered. St. Clair peeled off his shirt and let his underwear droop over his belt. Producing pigging strings, Upton turned to order the farrier sergeant to bind St. Clair, but the man was gone. "Now where in hell — no matter," he said, and tied St. Clair spread-eagled against the wheel, his bare back exposed.

Several troopers filtered up from the rear of the stable and stood in a loose group. Lieutenant Upton seized the whip again and flourished it. "This," he said, "is something you should all remember. I'm a fair officer, but I'll not tolerate laxity in my command."

Determined not to flinch, St. Clair jerked heavily as the whip laid a hot finger across his back, leaving a bloody welt. Upton laid it on with grim determination — five — six — seven — he counted with the breath whistling through his teeth.

When he drew back for the eighth stroke, someone grabbed the whip and yanked, jerking Upton so that he toppled into the manure and loose hay. With blazing eyes he turned to this meddler, then scrambled to his feet and a stiff attention.

Never taking his eyes from Upton, Captain Buckley said, "Cut that man down, troopers, and be quick about it!"

Three men jumped to comply. St. Clair sat down gingerly, his back aflame.

"Just what the hell's the meaning of this?" Buckley demanded and Upton swayed, paling before the winter wind of this man's voice.

"I — this man was insubordinate, sir. He refused to fall out for work call this morning."

"This-sergeant-is-assigned-to-headquarters-for-special-duty," Buckley intoned with slow clarity. "Didn't he tell you that?"

"Yes, sir. I thought he was lying, sir."

"You *thought!*" Buckley let this drip scorn. "Mister, no one accused *you* of thinking. As a rule," he added more calmly, "I don't reprimand a junior officer in the presence of enlisted men, but for you, Mister, I'll break that rule. You flatter yourself that you can think. I will inform you, Mister, that your infinitesimal intellect is incapable of even the most minute computation without error. You green, heavy-handed John! I was commanding a platoon while you were picking your nose in grade school, trying to cram addition into that rock head of yours. Now hear me well,

John! If I hear of you maltreating a trooper in my command, I'll ship you so far out into the Indian country *they* won't even be able to find you." He made a disgusted motion with his hand. "Now get the hell out of my sight!"

So great was Lieutenant Upton's fury that he wept openly while recrossing the parade to his waiting detail. Stopping at the horse trough, he washed his face and strained for composure. Never in his life had he been talked to like that. The effect left him visibly shaken.

CHAPTER 14

Alex Howison ordered breakfast brought to his room as soon as Wade Garland had mounted a livery horse and ridden toward the telegraph camp, twenty miles west of town. Garland's suggestion that Howison accompany him had been pushed aside with mild complaints of a bilious stomach, and Garland had accepted this explanation as he did most everything else Alex Howison said.

Over his second cup of coffee, Howison glanced at his huntingcase watch, then went to the door and gently slid back the bolt. He peered up and down the hall before going to a broom closet and opening it. Frank Royce stepped out, ducking immediately into Howison's room.

Howison indicated the coffee pot and Royce was finishing a cup when a soft rap rattled the door. Captain Ackerman entered the room, smiled when he saw Royce, and said, "Major, you worry the hell out of me sometimes."

"I worry the hell out of myself," Royce

admitted, and accepted one of Howison's cigars.

"I came as quickly as I could," Ackerman said. "Also, I spoke to Lieutenant Upton last night. Really, Alex, do we need this upstart?"

"He is a little overweening, isn't he?" Howison smiled. "Phil, he has a job to do and if I had to blow him up a little —"

"A little?" Phil Ackerman was shocked. "He told me he was going to command regiments — armies! He'll never make first lieutenant, let alone general."

"I know, I know," Howison said. "Some men you buy with gold, while others are content with promises. The point is, Garland is feeling good. He believes St. Clair's a magician who can dispel evil spirits." Howison glanced at Frank Royce. "You took a hell of a licking on the river, Major — and from a green second lieutenant."

"I'll make that up, sir."

"I'm going to give you the chance," Howison promised. "You know of Wycop? He's doing a thriving business in trade muskets. I've got him at the pole camp now; he works there right under Garland's nose. Since you're in civilian clothes now, I want you to join him. Identify yourself and he'll take orders from you. Now that

248

Buckley's going into the field, I want the Sioux stirred up again. With a good defeat on Garland's hands, he'll be ready to agree with me that we should string wire out of Omaha. Then I'll move our operations up there and we'll break Western Union. I don't like this fighting on split fronts."

"Western Union has a lot of money behind it," Ackerman said dubiously. "That tells in the long run."

"Not this time," Howison said. "The backers are getting nervous. They've spent a fortune and have nothing to show for it. A good licking now will break Garland's back."

"That sounds good," Royce said. He stood up. "Keep us informed, Alex. I don't like working in the dark." He nodded and went out, closing the door softly behind him.

Captain Buckley and the farrier sergeant helped St. Clair to his feet. Buckley was saying, "Damn it, couldn't you stop this?"

"What could I do, sir?" the sergeant wanted to know. "Hell, he's an officer. If he wants to shoot a man, then it's covered by regulations."

"Forget it," Buckley said. "I'm just blowing off steam. How are you feeling, St. Clair?"

"Creaky, sir." St. Clair looked at the farrier sergeant. "Did I yell?"

"Not a damn peep," the sergeant said with considerable pride. "You could have taken a dozen and then spit in his eye." He glanced quickly at Buckley and tried to cover the slip. "Sorry, sir. No offense intended."

Buckley dismissed it with a grunt. He was soldier enough to appreciate the enlisted man's intrinsic hostility toward the commissioned grades. It was basic, and he would have felt uneasy without it. It was always considered fair game for a trooper to put one over on an officer. This was a game played by all with intense seriousness and with no hard feelings afterward.

"Two of you men bear a hand here and help him over to the surgeon," Buckley said. "See if you can get that back patched up."

In the surgeon's office, St. Clair lay belly-flat and had his wounds rubbed with ointment, then bandaged. One of the troopers had brought his shirt along and he dressed, moving carefully although the salve took some of the sting from his back.

"You might run a little fever tonight," the surgeon said. "Try to stay on your feet and keep warm. The stiffness will go away faster that way."

"Thanks," St. Clair said and opened the door.

"Better learn to button your lip around officers," the surgeon advised.

St. Clair went out and walked slowly back to the stable to get his gear. He saddled and found mounting difficult, but once aboard he determined to stay there. Walking the horse across the parade, he angled toward the married enlisted men's quarters.

Peg Delaney came out.

He leaned forward and crossed his hands. "Peg, I'm sorry about last night."

"Get down," she invited, "and I'll fix you some coffee."

"Can't. Going on patrol for five days."

"Be careful then." She shielded her eyes against the sun. Standing in the doorway, with an apron over her full-skirted dress, she looked very lovely. He longed to tell her so, but felt that she wouldn't want to hear it.

"Is that all you say to a trooper when he takes to the field?"

She shrugged. "What else is there, Quincy? If an officer says 'charge,' you charge. All I can ask is that you be careful." She frowned at him. "What have you got under your shirt? You look fatter."

"Bandages." He told her briefly about being spread over an escort wagon wheel. "So you see how it is," he added.

"You're not going out now?" Her voice was shocked.

"Certainly," he said, smiling. "Save me some coffee because I'll be back for it." Lifting the reins, he moved out at a walk, riding toward officers' row as straight in the saddle as if he were in the Academy riding ring.

Passing Lieutenant Upton's quarters, St. Clair turned his head as the door opened and Glorianna stood framed there. Her lips parted as though she wished to speak to him, but she raised her hand instead. St. Clair gave her a polite nod, then turned his head on impulse to glance across the drill field. He found Lieutenant Upton's eyes hard on him.

Glorianna disappeared and closed the door. St. Clair rode on to headquarters and dismounted with painful slowness. Entering, he asked permission to see Captain Buckley and was ushered inside.

Breaking off his talk with a tall, blond civilian, Buckley said, "Good God, are you so stubborn you don't know when to quit?"

"Afraid so, sir."

"I'd already scratched you off," Buckley said, and then introduced Walt Hardin. Wearing greasy buckskins and two huge .44 Remington pistols, Hardin was a Westerner through and through, but without the mountain man's slovenliness. He was clean shaven except for a drooping mustache that had never known a razor's touch. He shook hands solemnly and read St. Clair with a glance.

Buckley drew down a wall map and began tracing a route. "Leaving here, we'll cut north along Big Creek for about forty miles, then swing toward the southwest. There's a Sioux camp about ten miles south of the Smoky Hill River. We want to look them over, talk a little, and get out alive — that's our mission. We'll take five troopers, and counting Delaney, Hardin and myself, we'll make a party of eight. By my calculations we can make a night march, bivouac at the telegraph camp, arriving at the Sioux village around sundown or early afternoon. That about right, Walt?"

"Jim dandy," Hardin said.

Buckley looked at his watch. "We'll move out in exactly twenty minutes." He returned to his paper work. Hardin nodded and went out, St. Clair following

him. On the wide porch, Walt Hardin relaxed and lit a cigar. He tipped his wide
hat forward and studied the movements on
the drill field.

"Move here, move there," he said.
"Seems like a man'd get tired of it."

"There's a purpose behind it."

"Sure there is," Hardin agreed. "But not
for me. Takes a certain kind of man to be a
good soldier. Like Buckley — he's all right.
As a rule I don't cotton to the Army, but
now and then I find one I like. Officers, I
mean."

"Enlisted men don't count?"

Hardin laughed softly. "Don't get mad,
but troopers are like cartridges. You buy a
box, shoot 'em up and go buy another.
Don't the Army do that?"

"I never thought of it in quite that way,"
St. Clair admitted.

Hardin smoked his cigar to a sour stub
and tossed it away. Sergeant Delaney and
four troopers came across the parade. One
of them led Captain Buckley's horse.
Major Baker came from his office to stand
on the porch and observe the mounting of
this detail.

Captain Ackerman rode through the
main gate. He looked long and hard at
Buckley's detail, then trotted to the stables

and dismounted. Captain Buckley emerged from his quarters and took the horse from Trooper Axton. Gone was Buckley's uniform tunic. Over his shirt he wore a fringed buckskin coat. His saber chain, revolving pistol and accouterments were buckled around his waist.

At his command the detail mounted informally and moved toward the main gate, the troopers automatically falling into column and dressing right. Walt Hardin was leading; Buckley trailed him by fifteen yards. Sergeant Delaney and St. Clair maintained a horse-and-a-half length interval, while troopers Carp, Axton, Wilson and Clayton formed a perfect square.

With the palisade behind them, Hardin led them through wooded country intermingled with fairly thick undergrowth, and across a plain where buffalo grass grew belly-deep to a horse. By staying out of the ravines they extended their visibility and on every side they could see vast herds of buffalo, lazy and phlegmatic in the noonday sun.

Hardin turned in the saddle and said, "There's your bone of contention, Captain — the buff'lo. Meat hunters are beginnin' to kill 'em off. Was it to keep up, they'd be gone in ten years. Indians know they can't live without buff'lo, and they'll fight to keep 'em."

Buckley grunted and gave Hardin no argument, for he well knew how the Indian fared when administered by white laws.

Through the afternoon they rode west, skirting Big Creek on the south bank. After a fifteen-minute cold ration stop, Buckley ordered them back into the saddle and they pushed on through the thickening twilight.

Hardin led the way unerringly to Western Union's most forward telegraph construction camp. They rode directly to the squad fire and dismounted.

The camp was laid out in a square of tents. A wagonload of poles stood by the telegrapher's shack, an opensided shanty on stilts. The cook tent was to the right of this, with a supply of wire stacked behind it. Several men were lounging near the cook's tent and a moment later Wade Garland emerged with another man following.

He recognized Buckley and smiled. "You're an hour and a half too late, Captain. The renegades who hit us are gone."

"What renegades?" Buckley asked.

Hardin pointed to a point beyond the reach of the firelight. Buckley saw the smashed and torn tents and the vacant area where the horse herd had been pick-eted. A group of men stood there with lan-terns and the newcomers could see the still shapes of other men on the ground.

"Two dead and two wounded," Garland said. "They hit us at mealtime, about a half dozen men. Stampeded the horses first, then made off with two wagons loaded with supplies." He paused to wipe a hand across his face. "The meat hunter says he recognized one of them. Wycop, a tough from town."

"We intended to camp here for the night," Buckley said, "but we'll only rest awhile, then push on. Sergeant Delaney, picket pins, please. No guards. Three hours here, Sergeant. I wish it could be more."

Delaney and the troopers led the horses away while Buckley squatted on the ground with Garland. "The meat hunter says there's a Sioux camp some miles southwest of here," Garland said.

"We're heading there," Buckley said. "If your wagons are there, we'll return them to you."

"Uhmm," Hardin said, "better not promise that, Captain. This might turn into a rough scout."

"It already has," Buckley said quietly, and spread his blankets.

Three hours of sleep was not enough, but St. Clair awoke instantly when Axton touched him. He finished the task of saddling, and waited for Buckley's command to mount. It came, and St. Clair stifled a groan as his back protested painfully.

Buckley ordered them to close up and muffle equipment, then turned the column southwest. The land became smoother, stretching into a thickly grassed plain.

At the point, Hardin rode carefully, his head weaving back and forth in continual search. An hour later there was a housekeeping stop, with a ration of oats, for the horses, then to saddle and onward.

A tinge of false dawn marked the sky when Buckley ordered them to dismount and lead for ten minutes. Weariness was beginning to weigh on the troopers and their steps lagged. The last two hours had been agony for St. Clair. His back was aflame and a dull fever burned through him, making his head pound with each heartbeat.

Once Buckley had dropped back to ask, "How are you feeling?"

"Fine, sir."

"You're a poor liar," Buckley said and touched the young man briefly on the shoulder before resuming his place by Walt Hardin.

Thinking of this, St. Clair realized that Buckley had the true 'feel' of a born officer, a natural compassion for his men that put their welfare before his. *If only he weren't so rule-bound and old-womanish,* St. Clair thought.

Recalling Hardin's remark about troopers being like cartridges, he wondered how Buckley felt, and then knew the answer. In battle there would be desperate situations where a man could be forced into a decision that he could not otherwise make. A break in the lines that had to be stopped with human flesh, just as a leaky water cask must be plugged with a whittled peg. Beneath Buckley's compassion lay the hardness that would allow him to give such a command. But he was the kind who could never shed the memory of such a thing.

The world became more evident as the dawn grew; a pink glow flushed up in the east. Hardin raised his hand and the detail formed around him while he spoke in an easy drawl. "Sioux all around here. Yeah, they seen us, but we been movin' easy and doin' nothin' hostile. Lot of sign, Captain. I'd say there's been white men through here — Indian ponies ain't shod. Wagons been here, too."

"What's our best chance?" Buckley asked.

Hardin rubbed his face and gave it some thought. "I'd say them's Garland's wagons, right enough. But I'd go mighty careful, Captain. Could be them Sioux is waitin' for us to show up. Could be it's worth a man's hair to go farther."

"Technically," Buckley said, "we're at peace with the Sioux and we'll try to keep it that way. What we want to find out is *who* is fighting Western Union. I want those wagons and the men who stole them."

"This is your party," Hardin said, and swung his horse into motion.

Because of their fear of ambush, the Sioux had set their camp on high ground, away from timber but near water. The buffalo hide lodges were arranged in a huge semi-circle, all opening to the east, with the mouth of the horseshoe facing in the same direction. The lodges were high and narrow at the base, the flaps large and long.

Buckley rode in under the guidon, leading his detail without hesitation into the center of the camp. The children and women hung back, but the braves — especially the young ones on the edge of manhood — dashed forward and made threatening gestures at the troopers. Each man rode with head and eyes to the front, ignoring the Indians completely, and this was a gall to the proud Sioux.

Studying them with an officer's trained eye for detail, St. Clair saw that the warriors wore strand necklaces. Only one ear was pierced, the earrings interlocked and dangling nearly to the shoulder. Their clothing was buckskin and elkhide with fringed leggings and a hanging breechflap on the outside. The bare upper bodies showed no self-inflicted mutilations. All the braves wore long hair, banded across the forehead, with an occasional feather.

He scanned them for weapons. Every man had a knife stick — three knives fastened to the tip of a pole. Some were scythe-shaped, deadly in any fight. The arrows, he noticed, were barbed.

The two wagons stood in the center of the camp. The teamsters sat cross-legged by the large fire, a rod away. St. Clair looked carefully at the four white men sitting there, then said, "Sir —"

"I see him," Buckley said. Frank Royce seemed unconcerned as they advanced. Buckley halted near the fire and dismounted his troop, ordering Axton to hold the horses.

Buckley made the lifted arm sign of peace and ordered the guidon struck. He spoke to a young brave in rapid Sioux, then explained to his troop, "This is *Tashunka Witha*, Crazy Horse, as he is known to us. He's young but he promises to be a great chief, so conduct yourselves with some respect." To Crazy Horse, Buckley said, "Who are the white eyes who eat at your fire?"

Crazy Horse made the sign for friend.

"Hardin," Buckley said, "walk over to those wagons and see what's in them."

Hardin approached them slowly and flipped back the canvas. "Mostly general supplies," he said. "There's two cases of Sharp's rifles here, Captain. Maybe a thousand rounds of paper patch ammunition and tape-primers." He returned to Buckley's side. "You're playin' this mighty close, Captain. I'd say to let the Sioux have the damn stuff. Be cheaper than losin' your hair over it."

"That's stolen property," Buckley said, locking eyes with Royce. "Then again, there's another matter that needs settling. Trooper Wilson, hand me your carbine."

Buckley pointed it at Royce. Royce stiffened while the other three men edged away. St. Clair saw the flinty light in

Buckley's eyes and read the restrained rage churning there. "Sir," he said, guessing Buckley's intent, "the man deserves a trial."

"And I intend to give him one," Buckley said flatly. "Sergeant Royce, I accuse you of pilfering government property, inciting to mutiny, committing an act of desertion and treason, and engaging in armed warfare against United States troops. For the record, I'd like to hear your plea before I execute you."

For a moment St. Clair thought Buckley was insane. Then he realized that this officer intended to enact justice here, in the enemy camp. With the coldest kind of courage, Buckley was ignoring the fact that Crazy Horse would kill him if he went through with it, yet he showed no sign of backing down. Here was a daring that left St. Clair breathless, making his own fence-walking bravado seem immature.

Royce seemed to think Buckley was bluffing. He said, "I'll gamble that you don't get away with this." The man had a cool courage that did not desert him. "You're in a bad spot, Captain. Put up the gun and we'll go separate. There's no sense in your getting killed just for the pleasure of getting me." He smiled thinly. "Besides,

I'm a major in the Southern army. I have the right to a court martial."

"There is no doubt in my mind," Buckley said, "that such an army exists, but I cannot officially recognize it. You think I won't kill you. You think I'm worried about Crazy Horse's reaction. Well I am, but I'll take the chance."

Frank Royce made a frantic stab for his pistol. Buckley's shot drove him flat. Buckley handed the smoking carbine back to Trooper Wilson. "Reload it," Buckley said in the same voice he used at the rifle butts.

The suddenness of this violence held the Indians motionless for several seconds and Buckley took advantage of it. His detail covered the three teamsters while he turned to Crazy Horse.

"This man was a criminal and I have punished as you would have done. The other three are also criminals. They will come back with me." Buckley turned away from the Sioux and walked over to the three men, Walt Hardin at his side.

"This is Wycop," Hardin said, pointing to a stringy man in a dirty shirt.

"Did you steal this wagon from the Western Union line camp?" Buckley asked.

"What does Western Union say?" Wycop

said. "You'll never get me out of this camp, soldier boy. Not and keep your hair, you won't."

Buckley spoke without turning his head. "Carp, Wilson — tie your horses to those wagons and take them to the post. Clayton, Axton, ride along as escort. If anyone tries to halt you, hit him."

The four troopers hastened to comply and an angry murmur went up among the Indians. Hardin said, "Easy now, Captain. Easy."

"Place these three men under arrest, Delaney," Buckley said.

Cursing, Wycop surged to his feet, clawing for his pistol. Walt Hardin whipped up one of his long-barreled Remingtons and laid it across the crown of Wycop's head. Sergeant Delaney disarmed the other two, then produced a rope. Axton was handling the ribbons of the first wagon and they rolled out of the Sioux camp, two mounted troopers following in the dust cloud.

This was a skittish moment for everyone, especially Crazy Horse. He lifted his hand to give a command and Buckley cut him short.

"Is the word of a chief no better than a child's? You swore peace with the pony soldier, yet you accept goods stolen from him. You call friend the men who rob the pony soldier. Speak, *Tashunka Witha!* Speak, or be called *Kum-mok-quiv-vi-okya,* Man-Who-Speaks-Two-Tongues!"

Buckley understood the Sioux and he knew that their honor came before all other things. He was placing Crazy Horse's honor on the block, challenging it.

"Take the men and gifts in peace then," Crazy Horse said. The words almost choked him, but he dared speak no others. "The pony soldier is a strong chief who defeats his enemies without battle. From this day on you will have a new name among the Teton Sioux — *Tashunka Kokipapo,* Man-Afraid-Of-His-Horses."

"Let's get the hell out of here before he changes his mind," Hardin growled, and Buckley turned toward the horses. Wycop was draped across a saddle. The others mounted and Buckley wheeled his command, trotting from the Sioux camp. He slowed to a parade walk and proceeded under the guidon until completely clear of the hostiles.

He spoke to St. Clair. "Strike the guidon, Sergeant."

They followed the wagon tracks, catching up fifteen minutes later.

CHAPTER 15

At the end of a two-hour march, Captain Buckley ordered a halt and short rations. The sun was a furnace and there was no breeze. Walt Hardin squatted, his long legs tucked beneath him. "I could just see my locks danglin' from a lance," he said. "Buckley, you sure play your games tight."

"That's what I get paid for," Buckley said.

Delaney and St. Clair sprawled in the grass a few feet away. St. Clair turned his head and looked long at Buckley. The troopers sought the shade of the wagons. St. Clair said, "Sir, what was that name Crazy Horse gave you?"

"Man-Afraid-Of-His-Horses?" He chuckled. "In an Indian's inverted way of flattery it means that the sight of my horses will scare the pants off my enemies." He bit off a piece of dried beef, washing it down with a swig from his canteen. He glanced at the three men tied in the saddle. Wycop was bent forward. Dried blood splashed his cheek. He had lost his hat and his complexion was sallow.

"Who are the two with Wycop, Hardin?"

"Seen 'em around, that's all," Hardin said. "Toughs come and go, Captain."

"When I go fishing," Buckley said, "I like to hook the big ones, not the ones I have to throw back. Ranier was a flunkey who took orders. Royce was in the same class. I'll not sleep good until I face the top man, the one who engineers this thing."

"You take care of him like you did that fella in the Sioux camp," Hardin said, "an' your worries is goin' to be over." He jerked a thumb toward Wycop and his friends. "What you aim to do with 'em?"

Buckley smiled. "Frankly, I don't know. Turn them over to Western Union for prosecution, I suppose, although nothing will ever come of it." He glanced at St. Clair before adding, "However, I've been exposed to the hare-brained tactics of Sergeant St. Clair, and some of it has rubbed off. By the book I should march these men to the guardhouse and forget them, but I'm not going to. I'm going to release them on the chance that they will contact the man I want."

"That will be risky, sir," St. Clair said.

Buckley smiled. "Getting cautious, Sergeant? Could it be that you're learning to soldier?" He shook his head. "I'll admit it's thin, but I'll take the chance. St. Clair, suppose I gave you a command in a voice loud enough for them to hear. Suppose I told you to ride on to the fort with the word that I've discovered the ringleader. After you left, I'd turn these citizens loose and give you a chance to follow them. If they contact Mr. Big, we can pull him into the open and take a look at the color of his hide."

"I'll go, sir," St. Clair said.

"Get on with it then," Buckley said, and St. Clair went to his horse. Mounting, he heard Buckley calling to Delaney. A glance at the three men showed St. Clair that they were listening. As he stormed away, Wycop and his friends stared after him.

Before he topped a small rise, St. Clair looked back and saw the three men leave camp. They lost no time in picking up his trail, so he turned and rode on. He held to a lope, covering ground, but he made sure that he left a clear trail for them to follow. Keeping clear of the rolling land, he skirted Big Creek.

Often he paused to scan his back trail. For minutes at a time he sat straight in the saddle, his kepi tilted forward to the eyebrows, the chinstrap anchored in the cleft below his lower lip. Then he saw them and laughed, wheeling his horse.

★ ★ ★

Despite the fact that she had been born to the Army, Peg Delaney always felt a ratgnaw of worry when her father rode out on patrol. There had been times when he returned tied to the saddle and out of his head. Twice he had come back riding in an escort wagon with two troopers holding him flat against his agony. But he had lived to go out again while his daughter stayed behind and worried.

Now there were two to be anxious about. Although her emotions concerning Quincy St. Clair were clear enough, she didn't know what to do about it. He was far too much like Jim Buckley in many ways.

During the early part of the afternoon, she cleaned her quarters thoroughly, thus gaining respite from her thoughts. But the house was small and the task shortlived. Taking her wicker basket, she tied a scarf over her head and started toward the quartermaster's commissary for the weekly rations. As she passed the officers' picket quarters, a door opened and a young woman called her name. Peg turned and said, "Yes?"

Glorianna smiled. "I'm Lieutenant Upton's wife. You're the sergeant major's daughter, aren't you?"

"That's right."

"Please come in," Glorianna invited. "The place is a mess, but I'm lonesome for company and I don't know anyone on the post."

After a moment's hesitation, Peg stepped into the room. *Probably wants me to do her wash,* she thought.

"I saw you talking to Sergeant St. Clair this morning," Glorianna said. "I — that is, we were well acquainted back East." She brushed her hands against her hips. "We saw a good deal of each other."

"Why tell me?" Peg asked. "Undoubtedly he's known many women. Was there something special about knowing you?"

Peg Delaney's frankness rattled Glorianna. Her chin raised slightly. "Perhaps," she said. "You knew he left the Point under embarrassing circumstances, didn't you? He ran away a week before graduation."

"I believe he mentioned it," Peg said, "but then, people often run away from things, don't they?" She moved to the door and opened it.

"Wait, please!" Glorianna said quickly. "I just wanted to tell you — he's not for you. He wouldn't be happy with you."

"I didn't say he would," Peg said, feeling a rush of anger. "If there's something on your mind, why don't you come out with it?"

"All right," Glorianna said. She dropped one hand to the growing curve of her stomach, then let it slide away. The gesture was subtle, one that only a woman would make and another woman understand. "He has money and background. You wouldn't fit in. I *could* have married him, you know."

"How interesting," Peg said acidly. "Was he very drunk when he proposed?"

High color vaulted into Glorianna's face and Peg smiled. Closing the door, she walked rapidly across the parade to regimental headquarters. Womanlike, she figured the time involved and was troubled by the answers. Glorianna had been Upton's wife a little less than a month and yet. . . . Peg swore softly to herself and entered the clerk's office.

"I'd like to see the major, please."

The clerk left and then returned, ushering her into Major Baker's office. When the door closed, Baker said, "Peg, is that worry I see in those laughing Irish eyes?"

She sat down and folded her hands in her lap. "I'm an old maid," she said. "I just realized it."

Major Baker laughed and brushed his mustache. "I'm a bachelor and I've had my regrets. But only occasionally."

Peg said bluntly, "Do you like Sergeant St. Clair?"

"Yes," Baker said. "I believe he'll make a fine officer, if he can bridle his enthusiasm." He smiled. "It appears there's been something going on around here of which I'm unaware." He paused to kindle a cigar. "Peg, I gave your father permission to marry, and when your mother's family objected to the union I transferred him and promoted him to corporal. There was every reason in the world to assume they wouldn't be happy — but I remember that they were." He paused. "What I'm trying to say is, I'm looking for an excuse to meddle again."

"I need help," she said quietly. "Major, don't you think he's a lot like Jim?"

"No," Baker said. "St. Clair has the same rash surface, but there's solid realism beneath it. Let's face it, Peg. There wasn't a sincere bone in Jim's body. He had dash and absurd courage, but no staying power. If you're doubting St. Clair's sincerity — don't. They're not alike in that respect at all."

"Thank you," she said, and left.

She skirted the parade toward the quartermaster sheds. It might be easy, she decided, to tell Quincy about Jim Buckley.

But what would he do then? She didn't know and this bothered her. She knew what Jim would have done in his place, and was suddenly afraid. She could not bear the thought that he might not understand. That she might lose him.

Riding at a steady pace, St. Clair felt the first indication of a limp, and by the time he sawed the horse to a halt knew for a certainty that the right foreleg had gone lame. Cursing his luck, he stripped off the saddle and equipment and hid it in a clump of alders skirting a draw.

Whacking the horse soundly on the rump, he drove him away and then searched for a place to conceal himself. The alders seemed best and he settled himself to wait. He had to have another horse.

The sun was hot on his back. He drew his Colt and checked the caps, then cocked it and lay down. Visibility was good for several hundred yards down his back trail. He hugged the ground and peered through the foliage.

The minutes dragged by, and then a horseman topped a small curve of earth, the other two following close behind. The teamsters rode boldly to the spot where he had dismounted. One of them said, "Hey!" and pointed to the scuffed grass.

Reading the sign, they reined in and began to look around. Wycop moved in a small circle, his gaze on the ground. None of the men was armed and St. Clair said loudly, "Throw up your hands and dismount!"

Wycop, the tall one with the matted beard, surprised St. Clair by drawing a .31 Wells Fargo pistol from beneath his coat and slapping a shot toward the thicket. St. Clair fired and spilled him from his horse.

The other two decided to bolt rather than help the downed Wycop, and St. Clair broke clear of the thicket realizing that he *had* to stop them. Crossing his left arm over his chest, he rested the barrel of the .44 there and took a clear bead. The Colt coughed and recoiled against his palm and a man threw up both hands, slid from the saddle and rolled in the grass.

Unaccountably, the other stopped his horse and came back. He was bending from the saddle when St. Clair's third bullet caught him and tumbled him to the ground.

Wycop was still alive. He was trying to roll over and find his fallen gun. St. Clair got there first and put his foot on it.

Pointing his pistol at Wycop's head, he said, "Talk, or I'll blow out your brains."

"Go — ahead," the man said and coughed. The bullet had caught him under the shoulder blade and ranged through his lung. "That captain — be dead — tonight. Crazy Horse —" He slipped off his elbow and fell back, dead.

St. Clair vaulted onto Wycop's horse, driving it into an instant run. The pounding pace set up a pulsing agony in his back, but he vised his jaws and kept on. He knew instinctively that he could never reach the post in time to get help for Captain Buckley, so he turned to the left, striking north toward the telegraph camp. From his present position it would take two and a half hours each way. He had to beat the clock and he thought he had the answer.

The horse's flanks foamed under the goading run. St. Clair knew he should walk the animal to conserve its strength, but haste kept pushing him on. He raised the telegraph camp a little over an hour later and stormed through, flinging off by the telegrapher's tent.

Garland threw back the flap of the engineer's tent and ran toward St. Clair. "What's the matter here?"

"I've got to get a message to Major Baker," St. Clair said.

"There's no telegraph at the post. One in town though. They could send it on by runner."

"How long would that take?"

Garland paused to figure. "The major should have it in twenty minutes."

"Fine." St. Clair entered the tent to speak to the telegrapher. "Can you send as I speak, if I go slow?"

"Best operator they got," the man admitted modestly. "Just fire away."

"Major Baker. Buckley detachment in grave danger of attack by hostile Sioux. Possible position south toward Pawnee River. Will wait in direct line of march to guide you." St. Clair wiped the sweat from his face. "Sign that, Quincy St. Clair, Sergeant."

The telegrapher rattled his key to the mute length of wire, then had the message read back to him. He slanted St. Clair a glance and said, "She's on her way, soldier boy."

St. Clair walked with Garland to the engineer's tent. Garland poured him a drink, then asked, "How do you know where the Sioux will attack?"

"Guessing," St. Clair said. "Buckley will

have to keep to the flats with the wagons, along the Pawnee. He'll make four miles an hour so that would put him about here at sundown." He slid a map around and pointed to the spot. "Crazy Horse is mad enough to make big medicine and fight this battle at night. I saw his face when Buckley took the wagons and the renegades. He was boiling."

"You don't think they'll wait until morning?"

St. Clair shook his head. "The teamster said tonight. That can mean only one thing." He pushed his empty glass aside and declined a refill. "Well, Mr. Garland, we got your wagons back. Royce is dead and so are the others."

Garland studied the young man. "St. Clair, I don't believe you like this job."

"Id rather be on a manure pile," St. Clair told him, and went to the tent door to stand. "After this is over, I'll be right back where I started. I still won't know who the top man is."

"He'll make a slip," Garland said. "No man can be that smart all the time."

"Do you have a good horse I can borrow?"

"Take your pick. There's three left," Garland said. He came to the tent door and stood by St. Clair. "Sometimes I wonder why I'm out here myself. All I've had from this job is trouble." He smiled. "Tell Buckley to submit a report. I'll have to show something to the board of directors."

"He sent you one, didn't he?"

"I didn't see it," Garland admitted. "As a matter of fact, I didn't know he'd written one." He glanced at his watch. "Sure you won't rest a while?"

"I have to get back," St. Clair said.

He walked to the other side of the camp, selected a chestnut from the picket line, saddled up and rode out. Wade Garland was still standing in the tent door. He waved once but St. Clair did not wave back.

CHAPTER 16

The din of a moving column rises like a pall of smoke to enfold it. Composed of clanking sabers, rattling bitchains, the squeak of leather, the sound swells over the heavier plod of horses' hooves. Ahead of the troop, the point leads the way, with the solitary scout guiding the column. By the commanding officer's side rides the bugler to transmit all orders through his C horn. The guidon bearer comes next, riding to the right of the ranking noncom. And behind this select group are arrayed the fifty-cent-a-day regulars, the hardtail troopers with their sweat-stained shirts and mutilated hats. Carbines slapping, sabers beating against the stirrup leather, they are the fist, the punch that wins battles and drives back the hostile force.

They marched across terrain that was flat and unbroken save for isolated gullies. Behind the column rolled the escort wagons, the supply wagons and two ambulances with the contract surgeon driving the first. Whitecoated like a butcher, he rode with solemn mien, for ahead lay brutal work with no surcease. He was a man who had learned to hate pain.

Lieutenant Upton maintained a strict silence, only occasionally voicing a necessary command. He knew the contents of St. Clair's telegram and was content to bide his time. His mind contained just one aim: the death of Sergeant St. Clair. Niles Upton had vowed to see to this personally before the night ended.

Nine years ago this May, Lieutenant Jules Buckley had shaken hands with his father on the greens of West Point Plain, his shoulder boards flat and freshly sewn on his tunic. Then he had boarded a train for Minnesota Territory.

He had never returned, even for a visit.

This fact caused him little regret, for in Jules Buckley's mind, being an officer was akin to a monk: each should dedicate his life to his chosen cause. When after six years he had been promoted to first lieutenant, he considered himself lucky. He knew capable officers with fifteen years' service who were still being called 'mister.'

He had his 'railroad tracks' now; the feeling left him dumfounded still. But the mantle of command had never been difficult for Jules Buckley. If his captaincy meant added responsibility he was more than willing to assume it.

Riding at the head of his small detail, he kept his eyes alert, turning occasionally in the saddle to look back. The usually stolid Walt Hardin was edgy and trying not to show it. Running over the morning's episode in his thoughts, Buckley reached the conclusion that Crazy Horse had given in too easily. Of course the chief's honor had been at stake but that was wearing thin, for the Sioux had been pushed too much and lied to too often.

Once, he reflected, an Indian's word would have been enough; but taking a tip in business from their white brothers, they had learned the value of pretense when a rifle was to be won, or a load of Army blankets to be gained.

Selecting the route due east, Buckley kept the detail to a steady pace, concerned only with covering miles and returning to the post as quickly as possible. Beside him, Walt Hardin rode with his chin touching his chest, apparently dozing in the saddle. He spoke from that position. "Captain, I've decided that Crazy Horse is a lyin' sonofabitch."

"I agree," Buckley said. Behind them,

Sergeant Delaney heard this and was troubled.

"You think St. Clair got through?" Hardin asked.

"He's capable. I'd say so, but I'm sorry now that I turned the civilians loose. They just might manage to do him in."

"That's been my thought too," Hardin said, and rode slack in the saddle.

"St. Clair is no fool, sor," Delaney said. "If there's a fight in the makin', I'll put my pay on him."

"So would I," Buckley agreed. He called to Axton who was driving the wagon in the lead. "See anything back there, Trooper?"

"Nothing, sir."

"When I see something, I worry," Hardin said. "When I see nothin', I worry like hell." He urged his horse ahead, scanning the ground, then wheeled back. "Tracks, Captain. St. Clair came this way all right. Those three floaters was right on his tail too, judgin' from the way they was runnin' the horses."

"Be dark in another hour," Buckley said. "Ride on ahead and see if you can pick up anything."

"I'll do that," Hardin said. He rapped his horse into a run, rode over a scant rise and disappeared.

283

Delaney said, "Sure is quiet, sor."

"Yes. It builds up like heat lightning before a storm." Buckley squirmed in the saddle for another backward look. He turned back as Delaney pulled alongside. Ahead, Walt Hardin was on the crown of the rise, standing in the stirrups waving his hat in a frenzied circle.

"Double time!" Buckley said, and put the spurs to his mount. Coming over the lip of the rise, he saw what Hardin had found and dismounted while the horse was still in motion. The two wagons rattled up and stopped.

Wycop lay on his back, sightless eyes staring. A few yards away the other two were almost side by side. The frontiersman toed one man over on his back. "Sure did a neat job of it. Remind me not to get in a shoot-fest with that fella."

"A running fight?" Buckley asked.

"He waylaid 'em," Hardin said. "Tracks under the alders there. Sign's a little old and some of the grass has popped up, but I'd say his horse give out on him. I could look around a little. If the horse went lame he couldn't have strayed far."

"Never mind," Buckley said. He pulled at his goatee. "I'm trying to figure out why he didn't come back and join the detail.

With these men dead there would be no reason for him to go on alone. Yet he did. He must know something that we don't know."

"Better not stay in one spot too long," Hardin advised softly.

"You're right. Let's move out now." He swung into the saddle. "Walt, take the point and see what else you can read."

With Hardin out front, the detail once again settled to a steady movement, driving away from the sunset. As the light died, small depressions loomed as dark as canyons and soon a gray dusk settled over the land. Coming back, Hardin wheeled in his horse beside Buckley and said, "He took off to the north. Seen his tracks and he was makin' time. That make sense to you?"

"No." Buckley stared into the new darkness.

Axton, riding on the wagon, craned his neck, then yelled, "Sir, there's a band of hostiles at our rear! I saw 'em dip over a rise!"

Buckley galvanized into instant action. "There's a draw ahead," Hardin said. "A hundred yards and a little to the left."

"Hoooo!" Buckley called, and the wagons lurched into jolting motion. There was just enough light left for them to see a little and Axton sent the team plunging down the bank, overturning the rig with a shattering crash as spokes and sides splintered. He jumped clear and then Wilson veered his team to miss the wreckage and added his own wagon to the pile.

"Break out the rifles and ammunition from those wagons," Buckley ordered. "Axton, you and Clayton take the south side. We'll defend from the north in case they try to cross."

Delaney ordered the surplus rifles loaded and distributed and the other supplies in the wagons banked to form a barricade. Each man stripped the equipment from his saddle: canteen, knife, boxes of paper cartridges and caps. Then they settled down to wait and the night grew very quiet.

Hardin wiped his face nervously and fingered his drooping mustache several times. He gripped his Remingtons, the pearl handles gleaming white around the outline of his hands. His Green River knife was drawn and sticking upright in the ground in front of him.

Straining his eyes into the night, Buckley understood this waiting game, for behind him lay fights with the Comanches in

Texas, and the Mimbreno Apaches around Santa Fe.

From the shrouded distance came the call of a bird. But every man knew instinctively that it was not a bird. From behind them came an answer, clear in the still air.

"The Sioux're goin' to break one of their rules," Hardin said in a hoarse whisper. "An Injun's got to be deep in medicine to do that."

"Because they hate night fighting," Buckley said, "they may not put their full strength behind it. It's a hope."

"Slim one," Hardin said. "Get set now." He had scarcely spoken when he raised himself and shot point-blank at a running shadow shape. The sudden blast of the .44 detonated a mass screaming as Crazy Horse and his followers charged.

Muzzles flashed and braves fell, and then Trooper Clayton sighed and fell back, dark blood seeping from a hole in his forehead. Buckley's revolving pistol pounded against his palm. When it was empty he seized his saber, skewering a brave who tried to breach their stronghold.

Sound rose in a wild din. The Sioux broke around the fissure and passed on to regroup and charge again. Taking a rapid count, Buckley found Hardin bleeding from a slashed shoulder, but the man was ignoring it while he crushed paper cartridges into the cylinders of his Remingtons. Winding his small mechanical capping tool, Hardin fed caps to each of the nipples and sank back to wait for the next attack.

The remaining troopers were using the breech-loading Sharps with tape primers and this nearly doubled their firepower. Buckley had a spare cylinder for his Colt and he slipped it in place and reassembled the gun.

"We can't keep this up long," Buckley said to Hardin.

"They lost ten by my count," Hardin said. "*They* can't keep it up either. One more pass, and if they don't make it then, they'll begin to doubt Crazy Horse's medicine."

From the darkness came a screeching call, and the Sioux were charging again, firing as they ran, the flash of their muzzles great blobs of brightness. Resting his forearm on the ground, Buckley answered these flashes with his revolver, seeing shapes falter and sink to the ground.

Hardin's heavy revolvers shocked the night with each detonation. Delaney worked his Dragoon Colt, blasting each time he saw a shifting target.

The wave broke, passing to each side, and Troopers Axton and Wilson had been waiting for this. Their carbines spat in relays. Each man had half a dozen loaded Sharps by his side which he fired, discarded for a fresh piece, and fired again. They dropped four warriors before the wave passed on and the night again swallowed the Sioux.

But the price for this respite was heavy. Axton fell at the last second, one hand pawing weakly at his chest. Then his wound spouted blood and he fell forward and lay still. Trooper Carp was searching the dark ground for paper patch ammunition although his left arm hung bullet-shattered and useless. He said nothing, but his breathing was a labored sawing in his throat.

In this small gully, not twenty yards long and three wide, the detail prepared for another assault. But they waited in vain.

The Sioux were silent.

"What do you make of it, sor?" Delaney asked.

"They're losing too many," Buckley said. "They'll wait until morning or else go back for more men. There must be thirty left, but not enough to take us, the way Crazy

Horse figures it. How's that arm, Carp?"

"It'll do, sir."

"You're a noble liar," Buckley said. "Help him, will you, Delaney?"

"Sorry, sor," Delaney said. "I caught a low one on that last round."

Buckley wormed over to the sergeant. The bullet had hit in the side, just above the belt, and from the angle of entry had ranged across his stomach, nearly cutting him in half. His bleeding was internal and hopeless.

"Just help me sit up," he said, "and I'll be all right."

Walt Hardin heard this and crawled to Trooper Carp. Away from the depression where these men huddled, the Sioux waited, firing now and then to keep them down.

Counting the score was disheartening, for two troopers were already dead, Delaney dying, and Willie Carp out of the fight with one arm shattered. That left Captain Buckley and Trooper Wilson as yet unscathed; Hardin's wound was slight and did not bother him much.

Hardin worked his way to Buckley's side. "Hear that shootin'? That's a bluff."

"The bullets aren't," Buckley said.

"They'll wait until mornin' now. When

the sun comes up, we're finished." Hardin drew one of his pistols and patiently recharged it. "As a guess I'd say that Crazy Horse is roundin' up some more braves. Maybe whippin' us will make him big enough to tackle the post."

"He wouldn't have a chance," Buckley said, then snapped his jaws shut, for he knew that with enough warriors behind him, Crazy Horse would ride through the palisade as if it weren't there. "It's quiet out there now."

"I'll take the noise," Hardin said wryly. He peered over the rim of their position, saw nothing, slid back down and rested his head against the earth. "What the hell am I doin' out here anyway?"

"Trying to build a telegraph line," Buckley said. "That's as good an excuse as I can think of. The truth is probably something else."

Hardin laughed hoarsely. "I never built a damned thing in my life." He raised his heavy guns. "These are the only tools I ever owned."

"Some men build with a gun. Others with shovel and hammer."

"Th' Bible says somethin' about a man livin' by the sword is bound to die by it."

"Never read it," Buckley said. "Army

Regulations are my bible. How are you coming, Delaney?"

"Still here, sor." The sergeant's voice was weak and strained. "What time is it, sor?"

Popping the lids of his watch, Buckley held it close to his face. "Nearly nine-thirty."

Hardin was quiet for a time, and then he said, "If St. Clair made the post all right, then the relief ought to be well on its way. Ain't that so?"

"I suppose," Buckley said. "I was thinking what a hell of a fire those wagons would make. Out here on the flats, I'll bet the point of the column could see it for fifteen miles."

"Damned if they couldn't," Hardin said, and moved toward them. The smashed wood had been scattered over the ground and he busied himself making a pile of it. Using some of the ammunition, he formed a loose pile of powder and ignited it. It caught with a low 'woof' and soon the dry wagon beds began to burn. The waiting Sioux began to yell and fire their rifles. Light mounted higher, spreading outward in a flickering circle.

Hardin moved back to his place by the rim.

"Think they'll come in now?" Buckley asked.

"Doubt it," Hardin said. "That light is bad for 'em, shinin' in their eyes the way it is. With our backs to it, we could cut the hell out of 'em, and Crazy Horse knows it."

"Let's hope they charge then," Buckley said grimly. He turned his head to look at Delaney. The sergeant's face was white with pain. "Can you handle your pistol?"

"I think so, sor," Delaney said, but when he tried he could scarcely lift it.

The hostiles continued to shoot but the bullets whined harmlessly overhead or thudded into the piled supplies and the troopers made no attempt to answer them. This went on for half an hour, and then Buckley grabbed Hardin's arm.

"Listen! That was a bugle — a C horn!"

The sound was faint, the lilting ring of 'Charge.' It swelled as it drew nearer until it drove back all other sounds. In a moment, the drum of horses could be heard when an ear was placed to the ground. Soon they were able to hear the distinct rattle of equipment.

A roar went up among the Sioux as Crazy Horse gathered his men and mounted them for battle. He left a strong party circling the depression. Trooper Wilson proved this when he stood up to cheer and fell back soddenly, a musket ball through his neck. Wilson twitched a few times and lay still while Hardin cursed vehemently.

Riding full-tilt to meet the approaching column, Crazy Horse had everything in his favor — the night, familiarity of terrain, and surprise. Biting his lip, Captain Buckley huddled down while the remaining Indians peppered lead at their position. Although help was close, he realized they were a long way from being relieved.

In the distance, carbines set up a sputtering. Then the bugler sounded the bleating 'Recall.'

Crazy Horse had smashed through the United States Cavalry.

CHAPTER 17

Sergeant St. Clair made contact with Major Baker's point an hour and a half past sunset, reported, and was assigned to relieve the point. During this tour he found it difficult to maintain the regulation pace when his every instinct was to gallop. But now that he was a part of the unit, he had to conform to general march orders.

He saw the fire, a winking core of brightness, and wheeled his horse, driving the spurs home. But after racing a hundred yards back toward the column, he realized that Major Baker had seen it too. In the distance he could hear the faint rattle of small arms fire as Buckley held back the Sioux.

The trumpeter sounded 'Charge.' Then came the sudden whoop of the Sioux as they raced for their ponies — and in that moment St. Clair made a most important decision. A small part of his mind acknowledged that it appeared traitorous. He could not determine what sense gave him the realization that the column was due for a smashing defeat; he simply felt it, together with a driving urge to reach Buckley's side. He had to prove something to Jules Buckley. Just what, he didn't know.

The chestnut was a magnificent animal. It responded to the spur with a burst of speed that carried him far ahead of the column. He knew there would be Sioux around Buckley's position, so he flattened himself against the stud's neck, his .44 Dragoon in one hand. Behind him, a mass of howling warriors bore down on Major Baker's column and the bugler sounded 'Rally.'

Near Buckley's position, the Sioux opened fire. St. Clair weathered the erratic peppering. He jumped his horse over the rim and flung off, amazed that he hadn't been killed. He saw Delaney with blood soaking his side. The dead troopers leered at him in the dying firelight and when he looked at Carp, he thought of that one night in Crystal City when Carp had fought his best without asking why.

Captain Buckley said, "How does it look out there, St. Clair?" He nodded toward the fierce fight Major Baker was making.

"Don't know, sir. I was out front and couldn't get back in time. You're in bad shape in case the hostiles move in, sir."

"They'll move in now," Hardin said. "Through the grass on their bellies — with knives and lances."

"And we'll be here," Buckley said wearily. He squatted, suddenly feeling his years. He was a man ill-used. His eyes were bloodshot and red-rimmed. Dirt made a mask of his face and matted his mustache and goatee. He looked at St. Clair. "You're a fool or you wouldn't have come here."

Away from them the battle raged and shots pounded across the flats. The strident voice of the bugle called to men above the din of battle. Men and horses went down beneath the Sioux knife.

"Then I've justified your opinion of me," St. Clair said.

Hardin brought their attention around when he said, "Look alive!" and shot the brave who leaped into their position. The wagon boxes were about burned out now, affording only a feeble light. Another brave leaped over the rim, knife swinging. St. Clair grappled with him.

He seemed almost eager to meet the enemy face to face and they thrashed on the ground while he fended off the stabbing knife. St. Clair struck the brave hard enough to stun him, then rolled away.

Pulling his .44 in line, he pulped the bronze face with one shot.

Hardin's shooting filled the hole with sound for a time, and when the silence came, it came as a shock. Three braves lay dead by the burning wagons. Buckley slowly withdrew his saber, wiping it on his gauntlet.

"Close," Hardin said. "They'll be more careful next time." He sat down as though his legs were melting wax.

Bleeding from a slice on the forearm, Captain Buckley sheathed his saber and reloaded the two fired charges in his revolver. Then he sat down and stared at a spot between his outstretched legs.

The sounds of the main battle were more organized now. The troopers were firing in volley. St. Clair saw Buckley's guidon on the ground and crawled to it. He raised it, jamming the staff end into the earth. Immediately it drew fire, the bullets whipping the cloth until it hung in tatters.

Buckley watched this and spoke quietly. "Every man who fights and smells death wonders why he, of all people, has to die so ingloriously. He wonders why he couldn't fight on the battlefield and hear the drums beat and the trumpet blow, instead of expiring in some forgotten gully. That's the lie we learn, St. Clair. That's what they teach you at the Point. But it never happens that way. I learned the truth out here. A soldier is trained to die. The question is, can he die well? Can he stand his ground and bleed when there are no flags waving? A man wishes he'd never discovered the truth, because dreams die hard and we have that urge to live so we can dream some more."

St. Clair raised his head slowly and stared at Jules Buckley. "I think I've learned something too late, sir. I've found out I don't need an audience. What I mean is, I came here to stand with you, sir, regardless of the damned flag."

Buckley smiled then. "I told you once I wouldn't want you in my troop. The memory of those words choke me, Quincy."

"Quincy?" St. Clair said. "Sir, I —"

"I hear th' grass cryin' again," Hardin said.

Buckley pushed himself erect, spinning around as a brave dived for him, scalping knife slicing. Four more Sioux followed and the little gully became an arena. Shots blasted men back, breaking them. St. Clair shot a warrior through the chest, then whirled to shoot the one who plunged a knife in Walt Hardin's back. Captain Buckley went down, a Sioux on his chest. Sergeant-Major Delaney spent his last bit of strength blowing the Sioux's head half off.

The remaining brave gave a final whoop and leaped for the edge of the sink, pausing there as St. Clair's bullet took him between the shoulder blades. The brave fell back and St. Clair seized a fallen carbine, crushing the man's frontal sinus.

Buckley stood up like a man in deep shock. He shook his head several times, then came out of it. Recharging their guns, both men took stock of their position. Sergeant Delaney was still alive. So was Walt Hardin, but both men were sinking fast.

"Leave," Hardin said. "Damn fools — to stay."

"Shut up about leaving," Buckley snapped.

"Go, sor," Delaney murmured, his head rolling weakly. He motioned, the barest lift of his hand, and St. Clair knelt beside him. "You took care of — her once. Would you —" His head fell forward and he began to sag. St. Clair laid him down gently.

"Git — unless you want — to die," Hardin said, and clenched his teeth. The lips pulled away and blood made his teeth dark like a man who has spent a lifetime chewing betelnut.

"We have a chance," Buckley said flatly.

"Not in — this hole." Hardin raised his gun. "Got three shots left. Skedaddle!"

Buckley had no choice. He said, "Walt, I lied to you once. I'm a stiff-necked Baptist." He hunched himself and went over the rim. St. Clair followed him.

After the initial shock passed, Major Baker rallied his men. He saw that the Sioux had the advantage and ordered his men to dismount and fight on foot.

The fire from the Sioux muskets was not particularly accurate, but it was withering in volume. Mounted, Crazy Horse had hit the column like a scythe, splitting Baker's forces and forcing them to fight on three quarters. Baker lacked the strength to do this.

Firmly establishing the bitter thought in his mind that this was one battle he wasn't going to win, Major Baker had the bugler sound 'Officer's Call.' When they assembled, he gave his orders crisply.

"Lieutenant Miller, form a flying wedge, mounted, and break their backs with a diversion. Pindelist, rally your men for a

301

frontal assault. Upton, take four troopers and relieve Captain Buckley and his detail. If they're alive, escort them free of the hostiles so that they may rejoin the command. Gentlemen, we're in one hell of a position. As soon as Buckley's relieved, we'll get the hell out of here and give it back to the damned Indians. Carry on."

Returning to his badly rattled section at the wagons, Lieutenant Upton drew four troopers from the fight. He moved out on the quarter, putting half a mile between himself and the main body before cutting to the right.

He approached as close as his prudent nature would allow. "Remain here," he said. "I'll belly in. Should we be in a position to effect a relief, I'll signal with three spaced shots."

He moved through the tall grass on all fours. After covering a quarter of the distance he stretched out and reflected on the fickleness of chance. Before him, and undoubtedly dead, were the two men he loathed more than anything on this earth. He hated Quincy St. Clair because, in his worst moments, St. Clair was a better man than Niles Upton. And Buckley's unforgivable words still stirred a rage in Upton whenever he recalled them.

Upton listened to the sounds of the fight, wincing as the sharp rattle of pistol fire came from the depression ahead. The shooting stopped abruptly and a thick silence fell. He wondered about it, and for a moment he toyed with the idea of crawling forward to look at the dead men. But he lacked the courage.

Letting fifteen minutes pass, he turned and crawled back, then grew bold and ran erect the rest of the way. When he rejoined his detail Upton looked like a man who had just seen hell.

A curt motion mounted his detail and a few minutes later he rejoined the main body. Major Baker was wheeling his horse, firing his pistol at the distant muzzle flashes. He saw Upton, and when the lieutenant shook his head, Baker ordered 'Assembly' sounded.

The dead and wounded numbered fifteen. The contract surgeon was a busy man, his sleeves rolled up, blood covering his arms to the elbow, and the aftermath of fight had to be contended with now. The Sioux had withdrawn, having lost interest in what was already a great victory for them. Along the line of Baker's command, the blind shock of battle was wearing off. Battle is a drug, deadening a man while he fights, but afterward there must be a balance. Weakness claims him, and his nerves exhibit wide fissures. He is a sick man in need of help.

The haste to assemble and vacate the field was almost obscenely frantic. Troopers scurried around, gathering horses, helping their buddies.

Major Baker wheeled near Upton and said, "Brutal affair. No survivors from Buckley's detail?"

"No, sir. All dead."

"Frightful mess," Baker admitted. "Buckley was one of my finest officers." He saw some detail progressing in a manner that did not suit him and rode off, shouting orders at the top of his voice, the never-absent bugler at his side.

Starting back slowly, the column was sore now, licking its wounds. For some, this was first blood, and it had been frightening beyond their wildest anticipations. For Major Baker, it was degrading to be routed by a savage who couldn't read or write.

The Army always took rigid pride in recovering its dead, but Major Baker did not want to risk his men in the dark. In the morning he would dispatch a detail to recover them, minus hair and hands and feet.

This was an Indian custom. The Indians believed that a man met his enemies again in the hereafter, and the wise brave always made sure his enemy had a handicap.

CHAPTER 18

Because Captain Buckley understood in part the savage mind, he was not surprised when the three remaining braves bounded from the grass like naked and painted hounds. St. Clair killed the nearest with a shot from his pistol, then locked with another. They panted and grunted for a purchase to kill.

Buckley was possessed with a great recklessness. He parried a knife thrust with his pistol barrel and slipped inside the brave's guard. He locked an arm around the Sioux's throat and seized the knife wrist. Swaying, trampling the grass, they fought, and then Buckley threw the Indian over his hip and pounced on him. He struck the brave with his pistol barrel and turned on St. Clair's adversary. Buckley swung his gun again, then stood back as the man wilted.

"Let's get," he said, and bent low. They ran for a hundred yards before halting for wind. The pitched battle between Baker and the main Sioux force was petering out.

The bugler sounded 'Assembly.'

"Over that way," Buckley said, and got up. They trotted toward the column's last position but by the time they covered a half mile the troopers were assembled and leaving the field.

Around them the night was still thick and the hostile Sioux were everywhere. Buckley and St. Clair hid in the tall grass. Riderless horses moved in a nearby thicket.

St. Clair said, "A couple of those horses, sir, and we'd be in style."

"Plenty of time now," Buckley said.

For better than an hour they remained motionless while the Sioux combed the battlefield, picking up discarded equipment, especially the government issue carbines. Finally they stormed away on their tangle-maned ponies, shrieking and yelling. When the sound died, Buckley said, "Crazy Horse and his bunch will be counting coup the rest of the night. We'll move in a large circle. The first man who catches a horse will come to the other. These horses are spooky so let's curb the bright ideas and do this by the book."

"The book suits me fine, sir," St. Clair said. He turned away but halted when Buckley said, "Quincy, how did you get to the post so quick?"

"I went to Garland's camp and tele-graphed."

"That's original enough," Buckley said.

"I got the idea from you, sir."

"From me? I don't understand."

"You telegraphed a report to Mr. Howison," St. Clair said. "You didn't have time to mail it."

"You're dreaming. I never sent a tele-graph message in my life." Buckley walked away after horses.

St. Clair stared after him, trying to straighten the facts in his mind. Finally he shook his head and carefully picked his way through the tall grass. Within ten minutes he saw the dark shadow of a pony grazing and used a soft voice and gentle approach to woo him. But once the grass reins were in his hands, he vaulted aboard and became a severe master. Gouging spurs and a commanding knee, he wheeled the pony and rode to-ward Buckley.

He found the tall officer without diffi-culty and once Buckley was up behind him, St. Clair rode off at a mile-eating jog. St. Clair said, "Should we go back after Hardin and the others, sir?"

"They're dead," Buckley said. "I hate to tell Peg about her father."

"I'll tell her. It's my place, I guess."

"Like that, is it?"

"Yes."

"She's a real girl, Quincy. I'll tell you now that I once loved her."

"I didn't know that, sir."

"A man's a damned animal if he can't keep his feelings to himself," Buckley said. "Make her a good man, Quincy. She's Army and she understands what makes a soldier go. When the system gets you down, get a bottle and take it home with you. When you pass out she'll put you to bed and never give you her tongue about it in the morning."

"You want me to catch up with the column, sir?"

"To hell with the column," Buckley said. "The post will be there when we get in." A silence descended, broken only by the soft clop of the pony's unshod hoofs. "What was that nonsense you were telling me about a telegram?"

St. Clair found that it wasn't clear to himself. "Mr. Howison talked once about the shooting of Ranier. He said you gave him a report before we started up-river. Or was it after we got here? I don't remember. Then Garland said he'd seen no report. I don't know why this should bother me."

"I gave Major Baker a verbal account," Buckley said. "Baker could have told him."

"That must be it," St. Clair said, "although I'd swear he said you, sir. I'll ask Howison the next time I see him."

The morning sun was a glaring ball half above the horizon when the remnants of Major Baker's defeated column returned to the post. Wade Garland and Alex Howison were standing on the wide headquarters porch, chewing their cigars. The officer of the day dashed across the parade and a quick guard was thrown around headquarters as officers gathered for a conference. Because of their position with Western Union, Garland and Howison were invited to attend. Outside, the post bustled. The surgeon had wounded to care for and a grave-digging detail was organized. Men had died on the way back.

Sergeants' calls pulled men to attention, forced them into the military groove, for routine was a safe retreat. Like spokes of a wheel coming apart, they marched to their barracks.

At the officers' picket quarters, wives peered anxiously toward headquarters, waiting for their husbands to come home. Glorianna Upton stood in the doorway of her drab quarters. On Suds Row, Peg Delaney waited, her eyes turned toward the main gate. She was Army, and she clung to her hope that there would be stragglers.

Her eyes searched the troopers crossing the parade, and when she could not find St. Clair, she knew a moment of real panic. She leaned against the door jamb for support.

Glorianna was not Army. Neither was she calmly disposed. She intercepted a trooper and spoke to him. After the trooper walked on she stood there as though she had heard something her mind refused to credit. Then she ran toward headquarters and up the steps. Two troopers stepped forward and blocked her.

Peg Delaney watched this before turning into her quarters and closing the door.

Major Baker questioned each officer in the order of rank and seniority. He extracted every small detail concerning the battle. Finally he turned to Lieutenant Upton, who had attempted the actual rescue of Captain Buckley and his ill-fated detail.

"I crept cautiously to their position," Upton said. "I thought it best to risk it

311

alone, sir, due to the intense hostile activity in the vicinity."

"I will see that your concern and daring is mentioned in the dispatch," Baker said, bored by these ambitious officers. "Get on with the report."

"Very well, sir. Arriving at Captain Buckley's position I found him dead, sir. The hostiles had evidently swarmed them just a short time before."

"Was Sergeant St. Clair also dead?"

"Yes, sir," Upton said. "I will submit a detailed report in writing sir."

"Thank you," Major Baker said bleakly. "This is an abominable mess, gentlemen." He fingered his mustache. "You are excused, gentlemen."

Past the outer office, a trooper raised his voice in stern reprimand. Then a woman's shrill protest broke through his rough tones. Major Baker frowned at this interruption and the officers halted, puzzled and curious.

The woman's voice rose again, near hysteria. Baker swiveled his head, grunted, and pushed his way through the waiting officers. He threw the front door open. "What in the deuce is going on out here?"

Glorianna broke past the guards, shoved Baker out of the way and ran toward her husband. She struck him in the mouth, bringing a spot of blood to his lips. "You murderer!" She hit him again. Upton seized her wrists but she jabbed him in the shins with her sharp-toed shoes.

"What is the meaning of this?" Baker demanded. "Mister, can't you control your wife any better than this?" Major Baker was on the verge of disciplinary action and Upton knew it.

"Sorry, sir," he said. He tried to hustle Glorianna to the door, but she fought him, screaming and cursing him.

"Murderermurderermurderer! I'm ashamed that you're my husband!"

"Just a minute here," Baker said. "Release her, Mister!" He took her shoulder and shook her. "What are you saying? Calm yourself and speak."

Glorianna glared at Upton, although she spoke to Major Baker. "He swore he'd kill him and he did!"

"What do you mean?"

The other officers were edging back into the room and Alex Howison singled one out, shooting him a worried glance.

"I mean Sergeant St. Clair," Glorianna said. "Niles hates him and swore he'd kill him."

"She lies!" Upton snapped. "Why should I want to kill an enlisted man?"

"Because you think St. Clair's the father of my unborn child. But you're stupid, Niles. He isn't the father any more than you are. He's a clothing salesman in Highland Falls, a nobody — and I wanted to be somebody." Her defiance broke. She leaned against the wall, crying in a lost way.

The officers present avoided each other's eyes. Major Baker was all business. "Mr. Upton, consider yourself under arrest. Captain Ackerman, I'm appointing you to investigate this matter. After you escort Mr. Upton to his quarters, take a detail and recover the bodies of Captain Buckley and Sergeant St. Clair." He stared at Upton and his eyes were spears. "Mister, your conduct is a disgrace to the uniform. In the event that we don't substantiate a charge of murder, I suggest that you tender your resignation for the good of the service."

Upton cleared his throat. "May I speak, sir?"

"No," Baker said flatly. "I'd just as soon not hear it." He flipped his head around as a quick shouting commenced by the main gate. Annoyance moved into his eyes and

314

he crossed to the window, saying, "Can't a man have a little quiet arou—" He chopped off his words and bolted for the front door. When he returned a moment later, his eyes were afire. "Captain Ackerman, place Mr. Upton in the stockade under an armed guard. The dead men, Captain Buckley and Sergeant St. Clair, just rode through the main gate!"

Major Baker then dashed back through his office, off the porch and across the parade ground. Glorianna pillowed her forehead against the wall. She did not turn around.

Captain Ackerman looked at Upton and said, "I have my orders, Niles." He summoned a trooper from the porch, relieved him of his carbine, then dismissed him.

Upton fastened his eyes on Howison. "Someone had better do something here. I want out of this."

"We'll get you out," Howison said smoothly. "Captain, you'd better take care of this before Baker gets back."

Major Baker returned before Ackerman could usher Upton outside. Buckley and St. Clair looked oddly at Upton who stood before Ackerman's level carbine. Baker touched Glorianna and said, "Return to your quarters at once." The girl nodded and went out. A moment later St. Clair looked through the side window and saw her running across the parade.

"Take the prisoner out," Baker said, and closed the door after them. He unfrogged his saber and placed it on his desk. Beside this he laid his pistol and belt. Facing Garland and Howison, Baker said, "Why are you gentlemen here?"

Garland took the cigar from his mouth to speak. "We have to make a decision, Major. Either push the telegraph through here or out of Omaha."

"And I'm convinced," Howison said, "that it would be foolhardy to continue here. You've done nothing to remove the hostile forces working against the line. Today you suffered a defeat. Even *you* should be able to see that, Major."

"May I speak, sir?" St. Clair asked.

Baker nodded.

"Mr. Howison, we've cleaned up this mess considerably. Royce is dead. So are the three men who were with him. He wasn't the top man, but he was a leader. I call that progress, sir."

"I must disagree," Howison said. "Really, gentlemen, we are getting nowhere. As far as I am concerned, the issue is closed."

"Very well," Major Baker said. "Now if you'll excuse me, I'd like a word with Captain Buckley and Sergeant St. Clair."

"Of course," Howison said, and the two men went out. Buckley sat down by the major's desk and St. Clair stood by the side window overlooking the dusty parade. Captain Ackerman and Niles Upton lingered by headquarters steps. Howison came out with Garland. This St. Clair saw at the extreme edge of his vision, for a wall angle partially obscured his view.

Ackerman and Upton started across the parade and when they were twenty feet from the porch, Ackerman stepped aside. Upton halted, turning on his heel. From the porch a pistol popped. Upton took one staggering step and fell.

Major Baker had been sorting maps and he raised his head. From the main gate, the sergeant of the guard shouted in a bull voice. "What's going on out there, St. Clair?" Baker asked, plainly irritated.

"I believe the prisoner has just been murdered," St. Clair said evenly. Major Baker stared, then bolted for the door. A guard detail clustered around Upton. Captain Ackerman was standing on the porch with Alex Howison. Wade Garland was there but he looked from face to face, a puzzled man.

"Sir," Ackerman said as Baker came up, "Lieutenant Upton made an attempt to seize my carbine. Mr. Howison saw it and shot him in time, sir."

"Is that the way it happened?" Baker was speaking to Garland.

"I don't know," he said. "Alex was out of cigars and asked me to walk to the sutler's after some. I turned away, took four or five steps and a gun went off. Upton was falling as I turned."

"You wanted your ringleader," Howison said, pointing, "well there he is. I've suspected him and was watching for him to make his move. When he struck Captain Ackerman, I took a hand. Men like him have cost Western Union too much money."

"Major Baker," St. Clair said, "I made a statement in your office. Are you prepared to believe it?"

"Yes," Baker said without hesitation.

"Did you give Captain Buckley's verbal report on the Crystal City affair to Mr. Howison?"

"No," Baker said. "What makes you think I did?"

St. Clair glanced at Buckley, passed a silent message to him. Then he flipped open Howison's coat, scattering three cigars onto headquarters porch.

Wade Garland said, "What?"

"A question has been bothering the hell out of me," St. Clair said. "How did Mr. Howison know so much about Crystal City? No one told him — at least no one on our side of the fence." He locked eyes with Howison. "You knew about Royce's attempt on my life because *you* told him I was an officer, a spy."

"This is *too* much," Howison said. "You'd better be able to prove this."

"I think I can," St. Clair said. "I was looking through the side window when Niles Upton turned." His glance swung to Ackerman. "Where did he strike you, Captain? In the face? The body?" His eyes whipped back to Howison. "Your hand was on your pistol as Upton marched across the parade. Were you afraid he would talk? He wasn't very brave, was he?"

St. Clair caught Ackerman's move out of the corner of his eye, but Buckley was already after him. Ackerman fired and Buckley grunted, stumbling slightly. Then he closed with Ackerman and they rolled off the porch. Dust boiled as they thrashed on the parade.

Crushing Major Baker into Garland, Howison ran along the edge of the porch to where the horses were tied. Baker fell but Garland rolled clear. His hand came up with a four-shot pocket pistol and he took a steady aim. The gun cracked and Howison paused at the edge of the porch, his leg extended to catch his weight. He fell and tried to sit up.

Buckley, with St. Clair's help, disarmed Captain Ackerman. Then Buckley braced himself on stiffened arms while blood began to soak his side. He unbuttoned his tunic and examined the ribs where the bullet had gouged a furrow. When St. Clair bent over him, Buckley said, "Go on, look after the big cheese."

Garland was standing over the suffering Howison, his small pistol still in his hand. "For years I trusted you," Garland was saying. "Put my faith, my money, in your hands. You're pretty low, Alex. A lot of men died because of your schemes. Your kind starts wars, then gets fat on the blood." He wiped a hand across his face. "I never shot a man before, but with you it was easy. I put that bullet in low and deep, Alex. The surgeon won't be able to cut it out either. You'll last a day or two, maybe three. Give you time to think."

He turned away and walked with stumbling steps toward his horse. Pausing with a foot in the stirrup, he looked at St. Clair. "A good job, Lieutenant. Sorry it couldn't have been a happier one." He swung up and a moment later the palisade gates opened for him. Captain Ackerman was standing between two armed troopers, his face bloody from Buckley's fists. Major Baker said, "Hearings will commence at ten sharp tomorrow morning. Good day, gentlemen."

St. Clair wanted to help Buckley but the captain pushed him away without anger. "You got someone waiting for you, Quincy. Get to it."

"Yes, sir," St. Clair said, and walked toward the enlisted men's quarters. Peg Delaney had stepped outside a moment after the shooting and now she watched Quincy St. Clair walking toward her. She understood that her father was dead, but she shed no tears. She had never worn a uniform or performed the manual of arms, but she was a soldier.

Her father had been a calm fatalist, a man who accepted the inevitable without worry. She supposed he was happier now than he would have been if he had lived to retire to his small farm — the one he had always talked about but never bought. She had discovered years ago that his dream was an excuse, his unconscious apology to her for the things his life in the service had denied her. And woman-wise, she had gone along with this deception to please him.

She supposed a soldier's dying was as natural an end as a man could expect. As St. Clair drew closer she saw a change in him. He was a man whose soul had been thrust into the flames and had been tempered by it. The brassy rashness was absent. In its place was a steadfast adherence to the 'system,' a confidence in it that would never again be misplaced.

On the plank walk fronting these identical quarters his boots thumped and he removed his kepi when he stopped before her. He looked at her as a thirsty soldier views his first whiskey since last payday. He said, "I'm sorry, Peg, but he didn't make it."

She nodded. "I know, Quincy. Don't be sorry, because he wasn't. I suppose I'll cry next week or next year, but not now."

He took her arm and went inside with her. He sat down at the table. "I was with him, Peg. He knew how it was between us." He touched her hands gently. "Peg, don't tell me anything about Jim. You never should have worried because I didn't want to hear it. What I'm trying to say is, don't push me away from you, Peg. This is our life from now on. No ghosts to bother us."

"Yes," she said, and turned away. She crossed to the stove. "You must be very hungry."

"It doesn't matter."

"I'll fix you something." She took food from the pantry. She needed something to do with her hands. He sat at the table, watching her. She broke three eggs into an iron skillet and laid strips of bacon around them.

"I'll report to the troop as an officer in the morning," he said, and tried to rub the ache from the back of his neck. "Buckley will be on sick list for a few weeks and I'll have to take over. Garland's got to decide where he wants to push his wire through. Major Baker will have his copperhead hearing at ten. Tomorrow will be a busy day, but it's a long way off."

He ate the meal and drank a cup of scalding coffee. When he pushed his plate back, she said, "You'd better lie down now." She came around to the back of his chair and put her hands lightly on his shoulders. He smiled and new lines formed around the ends of his lips. His eyes had a pinched look as though he had developed a squint. Getting to his feet was a slow process, requiring more mental effort than he realized. He walked into the bedroom and lay down on Sergeant Delaney's bed.

She removed his spurs, then tugged off his boots. She covered him with an Army blanket.

Across the parade, the regimental bugler blew work call, and he listened until the ringing tones died. "A pretty sound," he said, his eyes closed. Around him the Army hustled. Sergeants bawled orders and work details moved toward the hundred small jobs that kept an organization running. He was a part of this now. He belonged.

Tomorrow he would awaken and don a clean uniform with new shoulder boards. Tomorrow he would belong, but now he was a tired soldier. She closed the door gently to shut out these sounds lest they disturb him.

We hope you have enjoyed this Large Print book. Other Thorndike, Wheeler or Chivers Press Large Print books are available at your library or directly from the publishers.

For more information about current and up-coming titles, please call or write, without obligation, to:

Publisher
Thorndike Press
295 Kennedy Memorial Drive
Waterville, ME   04901
Tel. (800) 223-1244

Or visit our Web site at:
www.gale.com/thorndike
www.gale.com/wheeler

OR

Chivers Large Print
published by BBC Audiobooks Ltd
St James House, The Square
Lower Bristol Road
Bath BA2 3SB
England
Tel. +44(0) 800 136919
email: bbcaudiobooks@bbc.co.uk
www.bbcaudiobooks.co.uk

All our Large Print titles are designed for easy reading, and all our books are made to last.